Flames Of Fate

Martha Wickham

Published by Martha Wickham, 2015.

This is a work of fiction. Similarities to real people, places, or events are entirely coincidental.

FLAMES OF FATE

First edition. January 24, 2015.

Copyright © 2015 Martha Wickham.

ISBN: 979-8224806713

Written by Martha Wickham.

Table of Contents

Flames Of Fate 1

Chapter two 6

Chapter 3 10

Chapter 4 14

Chapter 5 19

Chapter 6 26

Chapter 7 31

Chapter 8 37

Chapter 9 42

Chapter 10 46

Chapter 11 50

Chapter 12 53

Chapter 13 56

Chapter 14 60

Chapter 15 63

Chapter 16 67

Chapter 17 77

Chapter 1 86

Chapter 2 89

Chapter 3 94

Chapter 4 97

Chapter 5 101

Chapter 6 106

Chapter 7 110

Chapter 8 120

Chapter 9 127

Chapter One Style

"Mom, I need a makeover. Can I get one?" Amanda called to her mother.

"You can as long as you pay for it with your allowance. You don't need one. You're young and pretty," her mother Alice answered as she played with Amanda's long light blond hair. "If you cut your hair you're going to be in trouble. Only a color and tiny trim, that's it. I have to go to work." Alice kissed Amanda on the cheek and left the house.

Amanda Violet Weaver was a good person on the inside and wanted her parents to notice how pretty she was on the outside. Amanda was sixteen and wanted a new image, she wanted a change.

Wanting to be made over to look like a model housewife she owned formal-looking clothes and wore low heels. Her biggest transformation would be changing her hair color. Amanda had her mother's permission to color it something different.

There had never been many rules around her house until her stepfather Mark Glass came, and he always seemed harsh. Before Mark, her mother Alice would work full-time and when she came home she cooked dinner for Amanda and was too tired for much else. Amanda thought her mother decided to marry Mark because he took care of her. She spent her time as a junior at York High School and doing chores around her New York home for her mother.

One February evening in 1970, Mark came home and found the house a mess. He yelled at Amanda to clean it up. He also grounded her from going out, unless it was to school, until the house was clean. She had no choice but to do it.

Before going to work on the house, Amanda stared in her mirror. Wanting a change she walked quickly to the drugstore to buy make up.

Amanda came home before her parents and went to work cleaning the house. She also cleaned her mother's bedroom.

Afterwards came her hair color. Having never done this before, she really wanted to go from light to dark, and did not want the kids at school or her parents to think of her as a dumb blond. Amanda did not think of herself in that way.

Amanda had permission to walk to the home of her classmate, Erin Horn, who lived three blocks away. Erin wanted to be a cosmetologist and planned to start her training soon. Erin charged a small fee to color Amanda's hair. Trusting Erin, Amanda agreed.

Erin didn't talk much except for the consultation. "I think you'll look best with brown hair. A golden brown that would catch any cute boy's attention. Let's do it!" Erin worked all the color into Amanda's hair.

Thirty minutes after applying the hair color, it was time to rinse it.

The phone rang and Erin had to answer it. It was her mother reminding her to do her homework. Finally, after talking for a long time, Erin went to the bowl to rinse and shampoo Amanda's hair color out the phone rang again, but Erin ignored it.

Looking at her reflection in the dark, her hair was brown like her eyes. After turning on the light it was shocking. Amanda's hair was actually brownish-green. Actually more green than brown. It looked dull and limp like wet cotton. It was weak and pieces were sticking out from hair that broke off and went down the shower drain.

Sorry for having bleached her hair and hoping she could fix it, she jumped out of her chair and started blotting her hair with a towel to dry it.

"The only thing you can do is wait a week then bleach it." Amanda did not have enough money to go to a salon and get a color correction. *Great, a whole week in school and with my parents, and I have green hair. Think of the humiliation.* The first thing Amanda did was put her hair back in a bun.

Amanda wanted to spend the school week with her hair in a bun, then on the weekend she'd try to fix it. Amanda didn't say much, but when Erin saw her she looked angry.

"What is wrong with your hair?" Erin yelled.

"Nothing. I never should have had you do it," Amanda replied as she ran out of the door without paying Erin.

At school the next day, her hair was up. She sat in the back of all her classes and had a good day until last class, physical education.

Amanda went into the locker room and changed into her jogging clothes. The class was playing volleyball all month. With her hair pinned up, she went to play in the gym. She actually liked playing volleyball.

One of the girls hit the ball over the net and she ran after it. Hitting the ball so hard, her pin came out of her hair and it came down. While covering it with her hands, the other team scored a point because she missed the ball when it went back over the net. Afterwards she put her hair back up.

In the next fifteen minutes, her hair came down twice. Bobby pins fell everywhere. Aggravated, she sat down on a bench.

Erin Horn walked up to her with some other girls and said, "Hey Amanda, is your hair green? You're not some kind of freak are you?"

Feeling defeated and angry because Erin was on the other team Amanda answered, "No I'm not. Are you?" Erin hit Amanda on her cheek and yelled for the teacher. "Mrs. Anderson, Amanda's hair is green and it's scaring me! Please do something about her. She's freaky."

"Amanda, go to the gym and then go home. And don't come back until you fix your hair. We do not allow punk hair color at our school."

"But I can't. I have a math test on Friday!"

"You're going to have to retake it when you come back." Amanda had no choice but to go home and bleach her hair earlier then she had planned. She stood up and walked out of the gym and slammed the door.

Amanda walked home, but didn't have the bleach she needed. She put off buying some until the next day. There were still three days left until Friday. The following Monday the school was having a Valentine's Day dance and Amanda wanted to be there.

Amanda had never bleached her hair before but thought it would be easy enough to follow the package directions. She got up and ran to the drugstore to buy it. Not seeing her mother yet, on her walk home she passed a movie theater. It was showing the movie *Countess Dracula* and she really wanted to see it.

After the movie was over she walked home and she noticed her mother's car in the drive way. "Amanda, why weren't you in school today?" her mother Alice asked.

Amanda knew this was the threat of getting in trouble she had wanted to avoid. "I got sent home yesterday."

"Why?"

"Because the PE teacher thought my hair looked offensive. I'm going to fix it tonight then be back in school on Friday."

"Rules were made by your stepfather. If you get in trouble at school then you're punished at home."

"Can you not tell him?"

"No, he'll figure it out tomorrow. So go get started on your hair then come to the kitchen for dinner. I promise he won't be too harsh."

Amanda left discouraged, looking at the floor. She started mixing the bleach and she shut the bathroom door for privacy.

Her mother waited for Amanda. Two hours later when dinner started getting cold, she heard her daughter come down the hallway.

Water was dripping off Amanda. Her first sight of Amanda's face had a frown. Her hair was like cotton and was falling out as she combed it.

After she finished combing her hair, all that was left were strands of over-processed hair.

"Come and eat before dinner gets cold. Then I'll help you fix your hair tomorrow after you give it a good conditioning. Don't worry, it'll be okay. You'll be back in school by Friday." Her mother was standing in the kitchen.

Amanda sat down at the table and asked, "So what's my punishment?"

"I haven't asked Mark yet," her mother replied.

In the morning Amanda's mother cut her hair. It was very short. Six inches to be exact. She quickly became used to having short hair and it made her smile. "Mom, did you ask Mark what my punishment was?"

"It's just the usual. You're grounded, so you stay in the house, and don't go anywhere unless it's with me."

"For how long? I wanted to go to the school dance on Monday."

"Then it will only be for one weekend."

"Okay, how does my hair look? I've never had short hair before. There's no green left in it, is there?"

"It looks okay, but just a little discolored. We'll put a darker semi-permanent color over it tonight."

"Good. This is the last time I color my hair," Amanda answered. She had learned her lesson about messing around carelessly with her hair. Still, she had many more lessons to learn.

Chapter two

Science Class

Thursday morning Amanda's mother fixed her hair color to a reddish brown and Friday she was back in school for her test. She ran home confident she had done well on it.

The following weekend she spent at home, but made good use of her time. She cleaned, did her homework, and cooked dinner for her mother. Her mother was glad and styled her hair for her. Amanda loved her new look and topped it off with sparkling glitter.

"Mom, there's a Valentine's Day dance at school on Monday and I wanted to know if you'd help me pay for a new dress?"

Her stepfather heard. "No."

"Why not? Maybe I'll even pay you back."

"Fine, then you can help you pay for it. I don't care. When will you find time to shop? You're not going anywhere this weekend."

"After I get home from school, I'll go and I'll have it by the time the party starts."

There was one thing left she wanted to do to top off this new image, get a date to the dance. There were plenty of cute boys at her school. She had met the only one for her and she wanted to see him again. His name was Richard Thompson. She was planning to ask him to the dance, but it was two days away and Amanda still needed to run into him. But the more she thought about him the more anxiety she had.

Richard worked part-time at a car wash, but since she couldn't go there, her idea was to run into him in one of their classes. Reality was, the idea made her a little nervous, but she wanted a date for the dance. This was because everyone else had a date and all the games and contests, she heard of were done in couples. Although sorry she didn't think of him until the last day, there was still hope.

Amanda would wait until the fourth period. It was science and she planned to sit next to Richard.

She ate lunch with her friends, Marie and Heather, and told them about how she wanted to ask Richard to the dance. "I'm going to ask Richard to the Valentine's Day dance. Do you girls have any advice?"

Marie, who was also in next period science class, answered, "He'll probably be there tonight anyway. Even if he says no, you can meet him there."

"Right, thanks Marie. Did you know I've had a class with him all year? I hope he takes me to the junior prom." Amanda wasn't finished eating when the bell rang and she had to get to class. "I'm not obsessed with him or anything; he just seems really nice and I don't know anyone else to ask."

Amanda and Marie entered the classroom together and saw Richard sitting in a front row seat. The teacher, Mr. Mason, started his lecture. "Today we'll start studying plant life, and next week we'll go outside and plant gardens. That's called horticulture. Open your text books to chapter four. We'll get started reading as soon as I take roll."

Amanda sat as close to Richard as possible, sitting three seats behind him and watching his back. As the teacher called the students' names for attendance, she wanted to try to speak to Richard.

"Hi," Amanda said as he turned around to the other students.

"Hi," he answered.

Desperate to start a conversation she said, "Do you have a pen I could borrow? I forgot mine."

"Sure," he handed her a pen.

"Thank you," she politely answered.

The teacher interrupted Amanda by speaking to the class. "Okay class, after we read the first chapter out loud we're going to break up into groups to do a quick quiz. You can make groups of five or less."

Amanda thought that meant she and Marie would be in a group together. The next group member would be Richard. It was a perfect idea for her to get to know him. She tapped him on the shoulder, "Do you want to join me and Marie in our group?"

"Yes, that's fine."

Towards the end of class the group moved their seats next to each other. "The first question is, what is photosynthesis?" Amanda asked this question already knowing the answer, but she was trying to get Richard's answer.

"I don't know, I think it has something to do with the sun giving energy to plants."

"I don't know these answers. Are any of you going to the dance tonight?" Marie asked.

They all nodded yes.

Amanda passed the quiz to Marie. She was distracted by giving all of her thoughts to the dance. "Richard, how are you doing in this class?"

"Fine."

"Then why can't you answer any of the quiz questions?"

"I can."

"Go ahead then." At least Amanda was getting some kind of conversation from him. "Can your girlfriend answer them also?" She asked him in a cute humorous way.

"I don't have one."

"Then you should go to the dance tonight with me," Amanda was finding Richard was someone who was easy to talk to, "because you can get in at a discounted rate if you bring a date."

"All right, I'll go with you."

"Can you be by my house at six?"

"Yes, I'll be there."

She wrote down her phone number and address and handed it to Richard. "Who are you going to the dance with tonight, Marie?"

"No one. I'll meet you guys there."

The bell rang for the end of class. "Bye Rich, I'll see you this evening. Here's your pen back. Thanks for letting me borrow it." Richard waved goodbye to her. Amanda was anxious about the dance, so the next two classes dragged. They seemed double the time they usually were. She couldn't wait for her date with Richard and she loved worrying about it.

Chapter 3

Valentine's Dance

Amanda's friend Marie drove her to a shop that sold formal dresses. She wanted to wear something that looked glamorous, but only went to the knee. She tried on a white dress and a pink one, but didn't like them. Finally she found a black one that was backless with rainbow-colored sequins; she bought it and black satin heels to match.

After getting home she only ate chips since dinner was at the dance. Her hair was in small curls. She had used a curling iron. To finish it off, there were two small red roses in the top curls. It was 5:30 p.m. And Richard Thompson was picking her up at 6, and the dance started at 7:00.

Amanda waited for Richard until 7:00. He's not coming. He didn't call me, either. Maybe he's not going to the dance. Maybe something's wrong. Maybe his car broke down," she told her mother. "I'm going to call Marie and leave. I'm already late. Well, I don't know if you can be late for a school dance, but I'm sure it's starting now."

Amanda called Marie, but she wasn't home. "She's already at the school Valentine's party," the voice on the phone told her.

Amanda had her mother give her a ride to the school. "I hope Richard's okay," she said in the car on the way there.

"He's all right. He must have just lost your number," her mother said while driving.

When Amanda arrived at the party she could hear music. She put a jacket on, and her wallet in her pocket, then got out of the car and waved goodbye. Stepping inside it was dark. There were candles lit on each table and spotlights in every corner. They were red and pink. Each table had a bowl of Valentine candy.

Looking around she noticed her friend Marie sitting with two other people she didn't know."Do you mind if I sit here?" Amanda asked.

Marie shook her head no and said, "Hi, where's your date?"

"He didn't pick me up. I hope nothing's wrong."

"That's okay. We can find other cute boys here and dance with them," said Marie.

"I don't want to. You can. I'm hungry so I'm going to the buffet to get something to eat." Marie disappeared into the crowd.

Amanda became bored and disappointed. That all changed when she saw Richard sitting at a table across the room. She jumped up, smiled, and clapped and ran over to Marie and grabbed her arm.

"Look it's Richard."

"Where?" asked Marie.

"There," Amanda pointed at him. She was suddenly excited and twirled around to the music that was playing. "I'm so glad he's okay. I'm going over there. She skipped all the way towards his table.

He glanced up at her.

"Hi, I didn't think you were coming, but I'm glad you're here. Do you want to dance with me? We can enter the dance contest," Amanda told him smiling. Before he could answer she saw Erin Horn. Erin was sitting right next to Richard rolling her eyes at Amanda.

Richard shook his head no. He wasn't talking much.

Amanda had the impression that he didn't care about going out with her anymore. That made her feel disappointed. "That's all right, maybe some other time." She appeared to have taken the rejection well, but inside there was anger and hurt. She forced out a smile, and then walked away.

Amanda sat at one of the dinner tables looking bored. "At least you're having a good time. When does this dance end?" Amanda asked Marie as she sat down.

"Not until midnight."

Just when Amanda thought she was calming down, she saw a sight that ruined the rest of her evening. Erin Horn was dancing with Richard. Amanda stood up. "That's it I've had it with her. First she gets me in trouble at school and now we like the same boy. I'm putting a stop to this."

"What do you think you're doing?" Amanda pushed her away from Richard.

"What does it look like we're doing? I get to dance with him. He's my date tonight." Erin kept dancing proudly.

"How come you never told me this, Richard? Were you too afraid?"

"During our science class I didn't know we were going together. My best friend had already arranged a blind date with Erin and I couldn't get out of it. Especially since he picked her up and then came to get me."

"You feel like you have to dance with her, too? Do I get to dance with you? I mean you look like you like dancing with her. She's a smart-ass and a bully, that's all. You must like trashy girls who wear tacky dresses." Amanda pushed Erin away again and tried to dance with Richard. "I'm warning you, Erin. Back away from him; he's mine!"

Erin stood there folding her arms. Inside she was furious and wanted Richard to herself. In a rage she grabbed a plastic cup filled with red punch and dumped it on Amanda. It didn't stain like she intended because the dress was black. Unsatisfied, she took another glass of punch and poured it over Amanda's head again.

"You rude girl! You are going to be sorry for this! Apologize to me." When there was no response Amanda turned to Richard. "Can I talk to you alone for a minute?"

He agreed and they both walked to the girls rest room.

"I can't believe you came with her. Why didn't you call me?"

"I didn't have the chance."

"Well, can't we go out some other time?"

"Yes, that would be alright."

"I don't want to share you with her. Dump her; she's a waste of your time. You see how mean she is? She's probably using you. Get away from her. Will you give me your phone number?" Richard nodded in response and grabbed a pencil off a table to write it down.

"Can you at least give me a ride home?"

"No, I came here with my friend Sam. And we'll have to take Erin back home."

"Don't."

"I have to," Richard responded and walked away to find his friend.

Amanda noticed Marie was watching. "You see how mean Erin is? She did this to me on purpose. I'll bet you she found out I wanted to come with Richard and went right after him. Can you give me a ride home?"

"Okay I'll give you a ride."

"Good; you can help me plan what I'm going to do about Erin. Let's leave right now. They were both tired of the dance and Marie agreed to leave with Amanda. Amanda wanted to get home and come up with a plan to win Richard back.

Chapter 4

R elationships

TUESDAY MORNING WAS cloudy and gloomy. Amanda missed Richard and wanted to see him. She didn't know Richard well, but she was already having possessive feelings for him. She rested on her bed staring at his picture. They had argued the night before, but Amanda had slept that frustration off and had forgiven Richard.

She didn't feel like going to school, but wanted Richard. When seeing him in the classroom she grabbed his arm. "I'm sorry about last night. You're not mad at me, are you?"

"I guess not. It was my fault. I should have taken you to the dance."

"I'm glad you feel that way. I wish you would have taken me. Maybe we can go to the prom together. I'll call you and we'll talk about it later." Amanda gave him a friendly hug and then went on with her school work.

The school week went by with a few angry looks from Erin. That was all of the attention she gave Amanda.

"I don't care if Erin likes Richard. I'm ready to fight for him," Amanda told Marie at lunch. "I called him and made plans to do some homework with him on Saturday. I'm going over to his house." Saturday before leaving his house, she kissed him on the cheek.

"I hope you don't mind, I'm leaving. We finished our homework early and I'm glad you let me help you."

"Do you want to stay and have dinner at my house tonight? My mother is cooking a big meal."

Amanda's eyes lit up. "Of course I do. Just as long as I can call my mother and let her know."

"That's fine." He brought her his cordless phone.

After dinner that night he asked her to spend the night. "You can sleep on our couch." They had gotten along so well at dinner and he wanted to watch movies with her.

Amanda agreed to this and called her mother once again. Late that night she felt like she had succeeded with him.

Lying on the couch at midnight, Amanda couldn't sleep. There was a drip coming from the sink and sounds of animals hopping around on the roof. She decided to look into Richard's bedroom and see what he was doing.

He was awake and Amanda sat on his bed. "You're not seeing Erin again are you? I don't like her."

"No, I told her we were just friends. She needs to find a boyfriend somewhere else."

"Good. I can't sleep out on that couch. Can I sleep on the floor in here with you?"

"Sure."

Amanda walked out into the living room and grabbed everything off the couch and lay down on a quilt he had on the floor.

"I'll give you a ride home tomorrow morning. Then I can pick you up and give you a ride to school on Monday."

It sounded like a good deal to Amanda. "I never thought I'd have a boy for a best friend."

In the morning Richard woke up and Amanda was sleeping right next to him. After waking up, she couldn't believe how nice he was to her. He even fixed her breakfast.

He picked her up for school on Monday morning as he promised.

"I'll meet you at your last class so you can give me a ride home." They were in his car. They stepped out. "My seventeenth birthday is April tenth. Do want to come over that day?"

Richard nodded, and then he walked away. As Amanda walked to her locker she passed Erin in the hall. "I saw you and Richard. Have you reclaimed your territory? You had better hope I don't claim him back again."

"He doesn't like you, Erin," Amanda responded. "I don't think anyone does. What are you going to do about that?"

"I'm scared already," Erin was sarcastically laughing.

"One day, you'll be sorry you ever met me Amanda."

"Probably." Amanda walked away.

At the end of the school day, Amanda met Richard at his car. Riding through the parking lot she saw Erin. As they drove by, Erin threw a small rock at their car. "She's not talking to you," Amanda told Richard.

As he dropped her off at her house he asked, ? think we?e known each other long enough to have a relationship. Do you want to be my steady girlfriend?

That was the question she had been waiting for. "Of course, she answered with a smile. "I mean, yeah, sure, I guess.

"I'll pick you up tomorrow. Richard drove away. Amanda was excited and skipped up to her house. In the evening when the stars came out, she thanked them for giving her Richard. For once her wish came true. One star was brighter than the rest. It twinkled in an optimistic way that gave Amanda a feeling of relaxation.

She spotted the Big Dipper and stared at the stars until becoming sleepy. The air was cool and quiet. Then a slight breeze blew over her mother's rose bushes and left a nice fragrant scent that put her to sleep.

In the morning her mother woke her up and found Amanda outside.

"What are you doing sleeping outside? You could have caught a cold. Don't ever do that again."

Amanda went in the house realizing she had slept a little late.

Thinking about Richard all of the time was wearing her out. She still loved him, though. On her bed she noticed some envelopes. It was her mail. Some of it junk, but one envelope was from Erin Horn. She opened it and read it out loud to her mother. She always felt safe with her mother. The letter said, "Dear Amanda, I want to share with you my true feelings. You have everything you want and now you even have the man I want. Richard should be with me and I want you to know I'm going to tell him how I feel. You should let him go to me, because he's going to choose me anyway. I know you think I'm angry with you and you're right. I have been since you first threw that ball at me in PE class. I hate your hair and I want you to stay out of my way. I also would like for you to show this letter to Richard. I want you to know I feel sorry for him. He shouldn't have to suffer through an unsightly girlfriend like you. At least he has me to fall back on." Amanda went on reading, "It was signed the other woman, Erin Horn."

Amanda sighed. "Mom I can't believe her. She wants to ruin my relationship with Richard. I'm not showing him this letter, no way. And I'm sure she won't get Rich. He probably thinks she's the ugly one. I'm going to make a wish about her. Then this letter's got to go." Amanda's effort to destroy the letter began. First, she put the letter under her mother's vacuum while vacuuming the carpet. When it got stuck, she pulled it out all crumpled. She put it in a fan that was on full speed. It only tore its corners. Her next attempt was the kitchen blender. She placed the letter in and put on the top. After turning it on, it was torn up more. She dumped out the papers and put them on her stove. Before the final destruction she swore, "I wish Erin Horn would disappear like this paper." Turning on one of the burners she placed all of the paper on top to burn. They caught fire then turned to ash. Amanda took a relieved deep breathe, dumped the ashes, and went outside to help her mother water the flowers.

Chapter 5

The Rival

Amanda and Richard spent a lot of time together in the next week. Maybe too much. Amanda even ate lunch with him all week instead of with Marie. After lunch they went to the library and then he would drive her home.

"I can't give you a ride home today."

"Why not?"

"I'm not going to tell you why."

"You're keeping secrets from me now?"

"No."

"I know you're not ditching me. Is this a sign?"

"No, I just can't take you home."

"That's just great! You're going to make me walk. What will it be next?"

"Don't give me attitude. I take it from everyone else and I don't need to take it from my girlfriend. I don't like it."

"I should have expected this. You never told me you loved me. See if I do anything for you.

"Okay don't get upset. I'll pick you up tomorrow. Don't be mad at me," replied Richard.

"Well you're right. I shouldn't be mad at you. I know you care about me," answered Amanda forgiving.

Erin Horn stood hiding behind books listening. She watched them both walk out the door and she wrote "I love Richard Thompson" on her note book and went to her next class.

When Erin got home it started to rain. She turned off all of the appliances so she could listen to it. She sat on the couch next to her window to watch it hit the glass. She held her kitten and petted her.

She was black and her name was Seana. Erin was alone, so she spoke to the cat. "I'll bet you're wondering why I want someone else's boyfriend. I guess that's because I've had a crush on him for a year and I can't help it. I want to break them up and it's not because I'm mean. It's because the relationship is worthless and is going to fail anyway. I feel a very deep friendly closeness to Richard." The only answer Erin got was the kitten purring.

Erin dozed off and the downstairs front door shut. She jerked, alarmed that there might be an intruder, but not scared. Erin liked to believe she was not afraid of anything and tiptoed as quiet as possible down the stairs to check it out. For protection she grabbed a poker that was by the fireplace. She noticed a shadow in the kitchen and raised the poker to strike the intruder. Feeling relief when she saw who it was, she dropped it. "Oh, Mom, it's you," Erin sighed. Her mother was one of the only people in the world Erin loved.

"Hi, Erin, sorry if I scared you. Did you already do your homework?" Her mother's name was Heidi and she had black hair and brown eyes just like Erin.

"I guess I did, Mother." Erin walked away to be alone. Erin was tired from a long day and wanted to sleep a little while. She went up into her room, shut the door, and the curtains. When she lifted up her covers she screamed "Eeeeeeeeek!" There was a large black spider on top of the bed. She picked up a shoe and smashed it. She pulled the sheets off her bed and tossed them into a hamper and picked them up to take to the washing machine. Entering the kitchen, she saw the cat was up on the dining room table eating her dinner. Angry, the hamper dropped and she pushed the cat off the table. She went to wash her sheets. After heating up a microwave dinner, she went to sleep on a bare mattress.

When Erin woke up it was midnight. She decided to sneak out and play a prank on her enemy Amanda. Erin wanted to feel victory like she had defeated Amanda. Wearing black jeans and a black jacket, she drove to her school to find Amanda's locker.

When Erin found Amanda's locker, it had a lock on it so she pounded on it with a hammer as hard as possible until the lock bent in half. After that damage was done she pulled four eggs out of her purse and threw them, aiming at the inside of the locker. For the finishing touch, she took a marker out of her purse and scribbled on the busted door. She reached in the locker and pulled out a notebook with paper in it. "This ought to be interesting. Amanda's personal writings are for me to read."

Erin was pleased about the damage she had done and was tempted to sign her name there but didn't for fear of getting in trouble. When she looked again at the notebook it was full of homework and notes. She put the notebook in her purse then rode back home.

She took one of her mother's beers out of the refrigerator and drank it. Feeling hungry, she decided to make herself a hot dog. Opening another beer, she poured it into the hot dog's boiling water to add flavor. Drinking the rest of the beer, she lay down on the couch. Afterwards she disposed of the cans in the neighbor's garbage can for fear of getting caught by her mother.

Before class started in the morning, Erin sat relaxing on the sidewalk in front of the school. She watched every student enter York High School. There were three little brown birds pecking at the street followed by five more that joined them. In the corner of her eye she spotted Amanda Weaver riding up the sidewalk on a bike she had never seen before.

The bell rang and before making it to class Erin saw Richard. She put out her cigarette and threw it away. Walking towards her class, she blew a kiss to Richard, smiled, and entered her classroom.

After asking the teacher if she could use the restroom, Erin snuck over to Amanda's bike. There wasn't anyone watching, and she took a knife out of her pocket. She cut the front and back tires until they went completely flat. After that was done, she ran to the restroom as planned and then back to her class.

After her class, Erin wondered over to Amanda's locker. There were a lot of people standing around it. Amanda was standing beside it with Richard. He was swinging the locker door back and forth holding a screwdriver while trying to remove it.

"Richard, can I have a ride home? My bike tires are flat and I can't ride it. I think somebody did it on purpose."

Richard nodded in agreement. When he walked away, Erin approached Amanda.

"I hope you know who's to blame for your locker attack. It's Richard because he's evil. You saw him trying to pull off your locker door. He's your boyfriend and he's probably trying to get back at you for some domestic problem you both have," Erin told Amanda.

"Also, his friend Tim told me that Richard told him he did it."

"Yes, I told my teacher, Mrs. Sage, about my locker but I don't think it was Richard. The person who did this should get a detention or two. If you know who did it just tell me. Now I have to move to another locker that isn't anywhere near my classes." She looked upset. "Richard said he was trying to fix my locker door but he couldn't and that's why he was trying to take off the door."

"Well, I've got news for you. Richard did this and he's going to get his punishment. Then he won't be mean to anyone anymore. I have to go so I'll see you around."

On her way home, Erin ran into Rickard. "I know you vandalized Amanda's locker. Anyone can tell that."

Richard answered, "So you know I got five detentions? Thanks for telling on me, but I didn't do it." Richard's face was pink with anger.

Amanda arrived at school a week later wondering why so many students were wearing green. "Why are so many people wearing green, Marie?"

"It's Saint Patrick's Day, you goof." Marie was laughing about it.

"Oh yeah, I didn't look at a calendar today."

Erin saw that Amanda wore a blue skirt and white blouse. Erin wore jeans and a green sweater. She approached Amanda and pinched her arm. "There's your punishment for not wearing green today, but Happy Saint Patrick's Day, anyway. No pain, no gain." When Erin left, Amanda whispered, "I can't wait until that one graduates." Her arm hurt where Erin pinched it.

Amanda did not know that Erin was standing around the corner and she heard what she said. Because of that, Erin had another plan to get back at Amanda. She had known Amanda didn't like her. She did not trust Amanda for that reason, so who would pay Erin back for her hurt? No one could and Erin decided that becoming aggressive would teach Amanda to stay off everyone else's backs.

That night after her mother went to bed, Erin got dressed for her attack. She wore brown pants and a shirt the color of charcoal. Her skin appeared to be the color of a withered leaf, and her black hair was pulled back into a ponytail. She snuck to Amanda's house five blocks from her own home.

In an insulted rage, Erin ran up to Amanda's house assuming everyone was asleep, and very quietly went to the flower garden.

She stepped on every flower, grabbed leaves and tore them, and pulled rose bushes out of the ground. She grabbed a big sharp round rock and scraped up the side of the car that was in the driveway.

Seeing how strong the rock was, she insanely banged the car window many times before it broke, opened the car door, and got in. Erin had found a set of keys under the front door mat and tried them. One of them started the car. She was glad she now had her own car and had a feeling of possession although it was not hers. She wanted to take the car and moved quickly to hide it out in her garage.

Before leaving, she threw the rock through Amanda's bedroom window and drove away.

Amanda looked out of her window and then came out the front door, but no one was there. The smashed flower garden and her stepfather's car were gone. Upset, she immediately called the police. They told her they would come over and take a look and fifteen minutes later the police saw the damage and filled out a report.

"If you find out who might have done this give us a call," the officers told her.

Amanda grabbed a camera and took a few pictures of the mess before cleaning up. She raked up all of the flowers and threw them away. When she was done, there was nothing left. The spot was bare with loose dirt and a few patches of grass. When the yard was straightened up, she went back in the house.

Amanda went up to her room and quickly put on shoes, because there were tiny pieces of glass scattered in the carpet. It was windy and cloudy outside, so wind blew through her room. Her curtains wildly flew in the air. Papers that had been blown around were all over making the room look a mess.

A sudden rumble of thunder was heard nearby. Amanda knew her mother would be home any minute and hurried to pick up all the papers. After vacuuming all of the glass, she took a big roll of thick box tape to tape up the glass on her window before the rain came.

The wind stopped blowing and the curtains lay down calm. When the front door opened, Amanda knew her parents were home. She went downstairs. "You're home late. I'm glad your back."

"Where's my flower garden, and what did you do with Mark's car?" her mother yelled.

"We were attacked. Someone trashed the yard and I called the police. Unfortunately someone also put a hole in my window. I didn't do anything with his car. The police said I should call them if I figure out who might have done this. I've got their phone number. You can call them and talk to them about what happened."

Alice took the card. "But where is the car?"

"I don't know. Ask the police." Amanda escaped the blame, but was grounded until she paid for another bedroom window. That was her stepfather's idea.

Her mother called the police and what she found was frustrating. The police wanted to arrest someone, but they couldn't say who it would be. At least not yet, because they did not know who had done the damage and taken the car. That was still to be discovered.

Chapter 6

The Hummingbird

At breakfast the Weaver family was quiet until Mark spoke up to break the silence. "Amanda, did you do something with my car? Why don't you get it back or pay me for it?"

"I did not do anything and I don't have any money to pay for a car. Your car insurance should take care of it." At that moment Amanda noticed that Mark was a little too worried. He was thirty, thin, and muscular, with brown eyes and thinning light brown hair. She was used to him though he was usually cranky.

"Are you sure you don't know what happened to the car?" Alice was only thirty-two. She had given birth to Amanda when she was sixteen.

"Of course I'm sure." Amanda sat quietly by herself at the table.

The house was silent, because her mother and Mark left. Suddenly there was a humming sound. It was very mysterious and she didn't know what it was. She walked through the house looking, but could not find it.

Standing in front of the open kitchen window and looking out, she saw the noise. A little hummingbird was feeding on an orange wild flower. It was delicate looking with metallic emerald green feathers and a long stick beak that it put inside the petals.

Amanda went outside to look. She hid behind some boxes in the backyard so the bird would not see her. It flew quickly and was hard to follow. It landed on a branch in the next door neighbor's yard. It flew and landed in the backyard landing on a pile of rocks.

The sight made Amanda sad and a tear came to her eye. The hummingbird flew away when it saw her approach. There was a nest on the ground and it was flipped over. There were two baby hummingbirds that were trapped inside. They were tired of struggling and were not strong enough to lift the nest off themselves. They didn't have a lot of feathers and their bodies were tiny.

Amanda lifted the nest and found an egg with a crack in it. It must have fallen out of one of the trees that were in the yard and the garbage from the garbage can had been blown by the wind all over the yard. She ran to her backyard and put on some gloves that were in the shed. She took a box, set it down, and called the local veterinarian to let them know she was coming.

Amanda grabbed the box and took it to the yard. She picked up the nest and put the eggs and birds in it. The nest went into the box, too. She took it into her house to wait for her mother to come home to take the birds to the animal shelter. While waiting, she put a small blanket in the box and a cup full of water for them to try and drink and pushed it towards them so they could reach it.

When her mother got home, Amanda explained and her mom was happy to drive her to the vet. They took the birds and left them there. The vet said that they would live. They were only starving and sore, but the cracked egg may never hatch. The birds would be nursed back to strength and health.

"We will be going on vacation to Connecticut on Easter for a few days, so plan on taking that week off from school," Alice told Amanda when they arrived home.

"Okay, I can't wait. Where are we staying?"

"At the Crescent Lodge. It's beautiful there. They have an Easter party and celebration there. Maybe we'll even go to church." This was only two weeks away, but Amanda wanted to be ready.

"Mom, I think you need to call the school and let them know I need a week. I can't do it."

Realizing this, Alice went straight to the phone and called but no one answered. She pushed play on their answering machine.

"Amanda, it's a message from Richard, come listen." Amanda ran over to the recorder to listen.

"Hello, this message is for Amanda. I'm in jail because I've been arrested for car theft and the vandalism of your house and locker. Call me back and I'll give you more information, the recorder beeped.

They both stood there staring at each other. "Oh no. I'll have to help him. He didn't do it. I'll just have to go down to the jail and tell them that. What is the number to the jail? Amanda grabbed the phone book.

When Amanda called, she couldn't talk to Richard, but made an appointment with Officer Smith. Her mother agreed to take her to see Richard and they left.

They went into the main office and asked to see Officer Smith. He shook her hand. "I'll take you to Richard Thompson if you follow me." They walked down the sidewalk and to the area where Richard was.

It was clear to Amanda that Richard was currently locked in a cell. She jumped with excitement when she saw him. At that moment, she loved him very much. It was his present harmless and helpless look mixed with innocence that she liked.

When she approached him, he looked tired, staring at the floor. "Hi Richard, how are you? Can I do anything for you? Can I bring you anything?"

"Hi, I'm all right, but I've been better."

"So what's up? When are you going home?"

I don't know yet. Next Monday the officers are going to take me to court for my arraignment. They want me to plead guilty but I'm not going to. You can come if you want. Amanda. I just want to say I'm sorry for all of this trouble. Will you forgive me?"

"Yes, I forgive you. You didn't do it, did you? And I'm sorry, Richard, because you are in here because of my problems. I hope you'll forgive me. Are you looking forward to pleading innocent?"

"Yes. I didn't vandalize your house or locker and I did not steal Mark's car. I am totally innocent."

"Will you write down the courtroom address so I can show up? I want to help you. I wish I could help prove your innocence, I'll try. I promise. But there isn't really any proof of your guilt. Just your relationship with me and your fingerprints on my locker."

"Amanda, you have to show up." He handed her the address.

"I'll be there and I'll bring you some books to read and some cookies."

"Time is up. I have other things to do. Let's go." Officer Smith seemed to be rushing them.

"Bye Richard, I miss you." Amanda waved to him, blew him a kiss, and left.

"Great, I guess there's a stalker after me," Amanda stomped her foot on the living room carpet. "What am I going to do? They might come back. I'm going to have to change my name to Lynn Robins."

"Do you want to stay home from school until the arraignment?" her mother offered.

"No, I need something to do. If I stay home in hiding it will drive me crazy. Do you really think I should change my name? No, that would never work. Maybe we should move then I'll change my name."

"We'll think about these ideas. I'll talk about them to Mark."

After Richard's arraignment, the school weeks went by fast taking Amanda's mind off of her problems, but she still was worried about the situation. The night before Richard was to go to trial, she was anxious and could hardly sleep. In her heart she held as much hope for Richard as she could force in, but reality showed her he was in a lot of trouble.

The thought of going to Richard's trial made Amanda nervous so she was glad her mother and stepfather were going with her. She did not get to tell anyone that Richard was innocent at the trial. The officers said Richard's fingerprints were all over the crime scene.

They also mentioned he was arrested when he was twelve for drinking alcohol and damaging a neighbor's home. His past record showed he had the capability to commit vandalism and theft. It was short and in the end, Richard received one year in juvenile hall with a chance for early release.

Amanda left discouraged. She waved to Richard again to make sure he'd seen her. He looked unhappy.

"I'm sorry I ever called the police now. I didn't mean for Richard to get arrested. What was I supposed to do, let someone attack our house?" Amanda asked her mother.

"You're right," Alice opened the car door.

"Now what are we going to do?"

"I don't know yet; we'll think of something to help him." Alice made that promise to Amanda.

Chapter 7

Vacation Time

Easter Eve came quickly for Amanda Weaver. All morning she teased her mother saying, "Happy Easter Eve'r Mrs. Weaver." She was looking forward to the vacation hoping it would cheer her up. Early in the morning she began loading the car with her suitcase and boxes that were packed with her clothes inside. Amanda rolled her eyes at the sight coming up the sidewalk. It was Erin Horn walking toward her.

"What are you up to? Need some help?"

"Sure I do," Amanda answered hoping for a peace offering. "Can you help me lift this box into the car? It's real heavy."

"How come your mother and father aren't helping you?"

"I don't know. I think their busy shopping before we go out of town to Connecticut," Amanda answered. She needed help lifting a heavy box that held kitchen dishes. "On the count of three, lift." After Amanda counted to three, they both lifted the box, but before they got it to the car trunk Erin's hands let go and the box dropped. Amanda slipped and the box crashed hard on top of Amanda's feet. She opened the box and dishes were broken.

"Thanks for the help," Amanda said sarcastically.

"If you weren't so weak this wouldn't have happened," said Erin.

"If it weren't for you, Richard would not be in jail. I wish you were the one in juvenile hall," Amanda answered in defense.

"I hope you have a rotten vacation. And you can shove your boyfriend problems," Erin said walking away.

"He's your problem, too, because it's your entire fault. And I think I'll have a great vacation," Amanda called out as Erin was leaving.

Amanda's mother came in from the backyard. "I just saw Erin Horn. She broke your dishes. She truly is a miserable person." Her mother looked shocked and angry.

"It looks like we'll be using paper plates on this vacation."

"Well, we need to get them now because in two hours we're leaving to get to the campground lodge by 12 a.m." Just the thought of camping cheered Amanda up. They were going to stay in a log cabin like a place that was out on a mountain. They were renting it from a holiday tour guide company called Mountain Retreats. By midnight they had arrived at their destination. The warm breeze of pine and quiet mountain air made Amanda relax.

In the morning when Amanda woke up it was Easter. Her mother had already made a schedule of plans for them to follow. Before they started, she called Richard to wish him a happy Easter and ask him if he got the card she had sent him.

Walking into the living room of the two-bedroom cabin, she found a basket of chocolate bunnies and candy with a card. After opening the card it said exactly what she thought it would say: To Amanda, From Mom. *Aren't I a little too old for this,* she thought.

The first activity on the schedule was church. Church had actually lasted two and a half hours. After lunch, Amanda went to the church Easter party. The most exciting thing she did was enter her name in a drawing. She did not know the prize, but the winners were announced before everyone went home for dinner. Standing in the church yard grass Amanda heard her name called. "Amazing, I hope I've won a diamond ring."

When Amanda approached the table she handed them her raffle ticket. They handed her a box wrapped in yellow wrapping paper.

She opened it and found a watch. It was charming because it was gold with an antique appearance. The watch was not new. It looked big, like a man's watch.

"Mom, I won a prize! Come out and see it," Amanda shouted entering the cabin.

Her mother came out from the kitchen; she had just finished cooking dinner. Her eyes lit up when she saw the watch. "It's beautiful, Amanda. I love it." She was admiring the watch. "You can wear it to the formal party we were invited to over at Mr. Sid's mansion."

After dinner, Amanda ran excitedly to her room. She didn't bring a dress because she didn't know there would be a party. She planned to wear her favorite blouse with her hair curled in small spirals and the watch on her wrist. By that time, Amanda's hair had grown back to mid-neck.

Amanda slept until the afternoon and when she woke she started getting ready for the party. Wearing black high heels and silver heart earrings and necklace, she rode with her parents in their car.

When they arrived at the mansion, Amanda was excited. Having never been inside one before she liked the feeling of being in a very large house. The outside was gray like cement and the window panes where white. It looked mysterious and sad, but beautiful. It was early in the evening and they would be there until midnight.

Not knowing anyone, Amanda wandered away from her parents to get something to eat at the buffet. There was a disc jockey there playing good songs but making bad jokes that were not funny.

Two ladies approached Amanda's table while she was eating and asked, "Can we sit here?"

"Yes."

"I'm Tonya and she's Kathy. Hi."

"Hi I'm Amanda Weaver. I came here with my parents." She noticed across the room a strange man sitting at a table staring at her.

She wondered what he wanted, but was distracted by the mysterious beauty of the mansion. There were bouquets of mixed wild flowers and a large crystal chandelier that hung above her table and sparkled like a rainbow.

"Do you know who that man is? The one sitting at the table across the room. He keeps looking over here."

"No we don't." Tonya was giggling. "I don't think anyone knows who he is. Ask Mr. Sid. Maybe he'll know."

Amanda got up out of her chair to the bar to get herself a soda. After sitting down to relax with her drink, the man that was watching her came into the bar and sat down. Noticing him, she became nervous and got up to leave quickly. In a hurry, her heel got caught on a table leg and she tripped falling on the floor. Amanda was fine but everyone was staring at her, including the man she was trying to avoid.

He approached her and grabbed her by the arm to help her up. Her drink had spilled on the floor. At that point, she started to become upset and a little shaky. The bartender tossed her a towel to clean up the ice and soda. Amanda was glad the glass did not break. "Thanks," she said. "I'm sorry." The floor was brown carpet, not tile, so it was a little harder to clean up. "At least the carpet wasn't white."

Sitting at the bar trying to calm down she felt the strange man's hand on her arm. He slid his hand down her arm and slipped off her watch. "Nice watch, Miss Weaver. Too bad it's not yours," the strange man told her.

"What do you mean? How did you know my name?"

"Because I read the guest list and I know your stepfather is Mark.

"I also say you stole this watch."

"No I didn't. I won it at church yesterday."

"I know you're not telling the truth because this watch was mine. It belonged to my mother. I mean it's not new. You can tell it wasn't bought yesterday."

"I didn't buy it. I won it at the church. If you want I'll have the church call you to prove that fact. Now give it back to me!" Amanda grabbed the watch out of his hands. Though it was new to her she was already attached to it and wasn't ready to let it go. "Can you prove it was your mother's?"

"I sure can and I will. I'll call your mother and stepfather tomorrow and we'll have a discussion about your behavior."

"Who are you?"

"Will Graves," he replied. "I'll be by your cabin tomorrow."

"Do you expect me to give you my watch?"

"Yes."

Amanda placed the watch in her pocket and went to look for her mother. She now wanted to leave. When she found her mother, she sat next to her for the rest of the night. Her mother made great company for her because she could always be comfortable around her. After they went back to their cabin, she explained what had happened with the watch and Will Graves.

In the morning Amanda was afraid Will would show up and start trouble. Her mother said she didn't know him, so Amanda planned to ask Mark if he knew Will Graves. When he came into the living room Amanda asked him, "Do you know a guy named Will Graves?"

"Yeah, why?" Mark asked.

"He accused me of stealing his mother's watch last night and he might be coming by today."

"Don't worry. Your mother and I will have a talk with him if he does. Put the watch away. We know it's yours." Three hours later, Amanda went to the church office to explain what happened.

"We're sorry," the church secretary Mary answered. "We're sure it was a donated antique."

"Will you explain the situation to Mr. Graves for me? I'll have him call you."

"Alright I'll do that." The church secretary was willing to help.

When Amanda arrived back home, Will Graves was there. "Here is the number for the church secretary. Call her and she'll explain to you that I won the watch."

Will, being respectful to Mark, agreed and took the number and left.

"Why did you let him in here? He's a creepy looking guy."

"We wanted to be friendly to him so he wouldn't give you any trouble," her mother answered.

"I can't wait until we leave tomorrow morning."

"You didn't enjoy this vacation?" Alice was pretending to be surprised.

"Maybe a little, but I want to get back home to Richard. You know what I need to do next? Help prove that he's innocent. It's partially my fault he's in Juvenile hall, and I'm going to get that Erin Horn involved, too. She may have a stubborn hard heart, but with some effort I'll get her to admit he's innocent and that she's the guilty one."

Chapter 8

L ost And Found

On Monday, York High School looked empty. For some reason not many students showed up. Sitting down next to Marie, Amanda seemed bothered. "I can't believe Richard's not here. Do you want to help me get him out of juvenile hall?"

"Yes, but how do you know he's innocent? Think about that."

"I will but you must think he's innocent too or you're no help. The first step is to get Erin Horn to admit some things. We need to find out her address. Okay?"

"Sure we'll work out a plan together."

"Keep an eye out for her and find out what classes she's taking. Better yet, meet me in physical education. It will be difficult, but we're gonna force her to help us and don't be afraid of her because I'll bring some mace. We'll see how the fool likes my volleyball in her face. Just kidding. Marie."

"I'm going to juvenile hall to talk to Richard before the junior prom since I can't go with him. Then we might sneak into the senior prom and meet Erin there. I know she's going and I want to spoil her night because I think she's the guilty one."

Before gym class. Amanda and Marie changed into their volleyball playing clothes. They went into the gym and started practicing.

I see Erin,"Amanda whispered to Marie. "While she's playing, let's go sneak into the locker room and go through her locker. Maybe we'll find her address.

"Okay. Did you l ook for it in the phone book?" Marie's hair was in a ponytail and her bright blue eyes sparkled.

"I looked and I couldn't find it. As soon as Erin gets busy, I'll wink at you then quickly get out of here. I'll wait for you behind the big locker room door."

"Right, I'll be there." Marie was tossing the ball up and down.

Glancing at Erin, Amanda saw her playing a game of volleyball and left the gym. Just as planned, Marie found Amanda standing behind the door. They both went into the locker room.

"I don't know which one is Erin's locker. Do you?"

"No," Amanda shook her head. "I've seen her in the corner over there. Let's look."

The girls looked but did not find anything. They sat relaxing in the locker room alone. Fifteen minutes later the rest of the girls came in to change because class was over. When they saw Erin Horn, they got up and ran to another corner. They watched as Erin went to her locker and finally saw where it was.

"It's too much trouble to search her locker. How are we going to find out where she lives?" Amanda whispered to Marie.

"We follow her home," Marie whispered back.

"Perfect, let's do it now. She's probably going home." Marie nodded in response and tiptoed over to her locker to get her purse.

Both girls sat outside waiting for Erin to come out. When she showed up, the hardest part was following her. They figured they would have a much easier time if Erin walked home and didn't drive. But unfortunately every day she would go to her mother's car and drive home. Their idea did not work and they only followed her to her car.

"She must live somewhere here in town. As much as I hate to do it, maybe we'll have to look in her purse to figure it out," Amanda suggested. "But we'll give it back to her quickly."

"How can she just let Richard sit in juvenile hall like that when she probably did it?"

"I say we scratch the idea of figuring out where she lives. We'll meet her at the prom, hide a tape recorder, and drag a confession out of her to take to the police. I'll call them and tell them Erin did it and then let them hear the tape. We will go to visit Richard this weekend and you can spend the night on Friday. I'm going to call to find out when we can visit him and bring him some chocolate chip cookies."

"Alright, that's a good idea," answered Marie.

Both girls sat quietly in Amanda's dark bedroom staring at shadows together. They were relaxing after finishing their homework. The house was still and quiet without a single sound. Her mother was not home, but out in Long Island for the night with her stepfather. Both girls had called off the idea of going to the prom.

"The heck with Erin Horn. I don't want to go to the prom. On prom night I'm going to be with Richard. What about you? Are you still going, Marie?"

"I want to go. I want to get dressed up," answered Marie.

"You're right, so do I. We'll get ready together, go to the salon to get our hair styled and then stop to see Richard before we go."

"Is he mad at you?" asked Marie.

"No, he knows his being in juvenile hall is not my fault. Do you know what the police told me when I told them I thought Erin Horn did it? They respected my opinion and said that they would look into it. I'll stop at nothing to help get Richard free. What else are girlfriends for?"

"You're right. Now let's bake some cookies." Marie stood up and went to the kitchen. When the cookies were done the two girls wrapped them up in a box with wrapping paper and a bow for a present. Afterwards they got ready for bed.

Amanda jumped up when she heard a bang in her backyard. When she looked at the clock it said midnight. Fear was in her heart because it was beating rapidly. She ran to all the doors and made sure they were locked. Walking up the stairs to the loft, she looked out of the window to find the sound. What she saw was not an animal. It was Erin Horn.

Amanda opened her mouth in shock. It was all she could do to keep from laughing.

Quickly Amanda ran downstairs to grab her camera.

Marie heard the noise and woke up. "What is it?

Amanda was already upstairs taking pictures of Erin. Erin was stealing tools and some small antique items, chairs, tables, and lamps. She had broken into Amanda's locked shed.

Amanda couldn't believe it. After the last picture the flash brightly shone out the window and Amanda ducked beneath it.

Erin stood looking around for the light, but assumed it was the porch light flickering. Amanda peeked back through the window and Erin was still down there.

Marie walked in wearing a white nightgown and looked through the window. "Erin's freaky don't you think? It's like her last name Horn is related to the devil or something."

"I know. When she graduates next month you and I are going to throw a party." Amanda felt nervous.

"I'm calling the police." Amanda called the police, but they didn't come out to her house for thirty minutes and Erin was gone when they arrived.

Early in the morning, Amanda and Marie went to visit Richard. "We're going to prove that you're innocent." They told him what Erin had done the night before.

"We're developing the pictures of Erin as soon as we leave," Amanda told Richard. "Here, I made you cookies. Don't worry, you'll be out of here in a few days. After the police arrest Erin, I hope they give her a lie detector test. When she fails, they'll let you out, I just know it." She kissed him on the hand. "Can I visit you on prom night?"

"Yes of course you can if it's a visiting day," Richard answered.

"Just make sure Erin doesn't find out where Marie lives."

"We won't let her figure that out. Do you want to get married next year after we graduate? I can start planning for a wedding now. Ha ha," laughed Amanda "I'm just kidding."

Richard then hugged Amanda goodbye. He didn't think Amanda was really kidding. He didn't mind because he was falling in love with the girl who was probably his only hope of getting out of his cell any time soon.

Chapter 9

Erin's Karma

Erin explained to her mother that she had bought the antique items from her friend. She was lucky her mother believed her lie.

"Ouch!" Erin dropped a dish and it broke.

"What happened?" her mother asked.

"I'm having pains in my wrist."

"Take aspirin and get some rest. I'll finish the dishes." Her mother took over the job.

Erin did just what her mother told her, but could not sleep because it still hurt. "Mom, my hand hurts too much to sleep."

"What's wrong with your hand?"

"Last night when I was at my friend's house, I was opening her shed for her when the door got stuck. So I pulled on it as hard as I could and when I slipped, I hit my wrist on a rusty nail and cut myself. There was a loud bang that scared me because I thought I woke up the neighbors. "See," Erin lifted up her sleeve and showed it to her mother. It was scabbed, swollen, purple, pink, and black.

"Look at that! It's still dirty," Heidi noticed there was still rust under the skin. "Go to the bathroom and wash it with soap right now.

Erin did what her mother wanted and taped a bag of ice to her wrist. Still unable to sleep with a frozen wrist she listened to music until the ice melted.

When her mother came in to check on Erin, she was asleep, and when morning came Heidi didn't plan on waking her up for church. Heidi noticed Erin's wrist was still swollen and bleeding a little.

"I wonder what was wrong with that door. Which friend did you say it was?" Erin's mother asked that afternoon when Erin woke up.

"It was Abigail Anderson," Erin gave her the name of a different girl she went to school with. She lied because she did not want to get caught stealing.

"I guess it wasn't her fault," her mother said. "How do you feel?"

"I feel bad and my hand is feeling stiff except for an occasional muscle spasm. This is terrible. I think I need stitches. I should call Abigail today and tell what happened to my hand."

"You can stay home from school tomorrow if you want to," Heidi offered.

Erin stayed home Monday morning, being given the chance to rest. In fact, she didn't go to school all week and wasn't getting better. By Friday her jaw was stiffening and opened only enough for her to eat. Her wrist was in so much pain that she could not hold a pencil.

Her friend Abigail was bringing her flowers, cards, and aspirin every day. Abigail lived close, just down the street. Most of the time Erin was in bed and had a fever. Her mother told Erin that she would have to take her to the doctor the next day. At that point Erin was sorry she ever broke into the shed and never wanted to see it again.

She felt she had learned her lesson and went on trying to forgive herself.

Erin did not have much use for the antique furniture, but thought it was pretty. First she wanted to sell it but was worried about getting caught. Eventually she stored it in the attic.

"Why don't I hate you like I hate Amanda?" Erin asked the furniture.

Erin put one of her old dolls in the chair and spoke to it. "I don't have a crush on Richard anymore and I am going to find my own boyfriend. If I loved him, do you think I would have had him put in juvenile hall? No."

Her mother walked in. "Feeling better? You still have to go to the doctor tomorrow."

Heidi and Erin went to this medical office for the first time. They didn't know which doctor they would get and they didn't care. After looking Erin over, Doctor Wheeler said, "It might be the flu, but I'm not sure."

A nurse came in and took her blood sample. We'll call you in a few days after we get the results. Here are your antibiotics." She handed Erin some medication and asked when her last tetanus shot was. Erin told the nurse she never had one.

"I'm glad this happened at the end of the school year. I can still graduate because I've already taken all of my tests," Erin told her mother.

Erin decided to go to school to clean out her locker. She wasn't feeling too sick to do that. Graduation was two weeks away and she wanted to make sure she had enough strength. She left the school feeling happy and proud that high school was finished.

When she walked in the door, her mother was waiting for her.

"Erin the doctor called. You're not okay, but don't get upset. Sit down. You only have a mild case of tetanus. As soon as possible, the doctors want to operate on your wrist and remove the bacteria. You will need to get two shots a day for four weeks, and take medication. How do you feel?"

"Well I was happy just a second ago. Now I find out I need an operation."

"There's no saying no. It's important to your health. Don't worry; it's just in your wrist. By the looks of it, I can tell you need to have it taken care of as soon as possible."

"Will I be out of the hospital in time for graduation?"

"I'll make sure that you are. After these treatments you should feel even better for you graduation."

"That stupid shed. I should've known this would happen. But of course I didn't. Do I get all the ice cream and flower baskets I can stand?"

"Yes, I'll buy you ice cream. I'll buy you anything you want." After this discussion the room was still.

"Am I going to die?"

"No absolutely not," Heidi answered.

The following days crept by slow as Erin sickly but patiently waited for her surgery. When the day came, Erin didn't say anything.

She crawled into her mother's car and went to the hospital. She checked in and watched TV until it was time for her operation. Given the choice to stay awake and have a shot or have the operation asleep, she chose sleep.

Erin woke up the next morning glad that the operation was over. She looked at her hand. It was stitched up where the bacteria was drained, and she felt a little dizzy from the drugs that were given to her. One of them was a morphine shot to kill the left-over surgery pain. She remained in the hospital for two more days and was proud of how quickly she regained her strength.

Chapter 10

Validation

Amanda Weaver wanted to help prove Richard's innocence. Richard's lawyer had gotten him another hearing. When the day came for his court appearance, she wanted to be successful. She was determined and confident since she felt the police were siding with her.

Erin Horn already had graduated and was ready to be arrested, only she did not know it yet.

"She has what?" Amanda asked Marie in her living room on the couch.

"Tetanus, she's already been through surgery and doctors say she's doing better, but she still looks a little sick. I saw her pick up her diploma on graduation,"

"That's so sad," Amanda felt her heart drop to her feet and a tear came to her eye. "I have such a tender heart for the sick." When finding out this news, Amanda was not as excited to have Erin arrested. Actually she wanted to drop the charges out of just pure sympathy. Forgiveness started to fill her heart, until she remembered that Richard was locked up for something Erin did.

"She's not going to die is she?"

"I don't think so," Marie was sipping on her glass of Coke. The phone rang.

"Marie, my mother just called and there's a hearing next week, June 23. Erin was just arrested. I hope she's taking a lie detector test."

"What did the police say about the pictures you took of her? Do they count for good evidence?"

"I don't know. I haven't showed them yet. Why don't you come with me to the court? I'll pick you up before I go. I don't want to go alone."

That evening while Amanda sat with her mother on their couch, there was a knock at the door. Amanda got up to look through the peep hole and it was Heidi Horn, Erin's mom.

"I just wanted to talk to you before court tomorrow. I don't think my daughter vandalized your house. She's arrested now for nothing and if she thinks Richard should be in juvenile hall for the crime then he should be."

"The judge will decide tomorrow who's guilty and who's innocent," Amanda replied.

"He already has and it's Richard who's guilty." Heidi did not know the truth.

"Not this time. This is a special hearing and we need to see the results of their lie detector tests. I strongly feel Erin has done this. She is the one who threatens me, not Richard. And there's one last overlooked piece of evidence you might want to choke on. I have pictures of her breaking into our shed." Amanda reached into her desk across the room and took out a few of the pictures.

"See these beauties," Amanda handed the pictures to Heidi. They were of Erin taking furniture from the shed.

"How do we know she's stealing in these pictures?" Heidi asked.

"I have more of her beating on the shed door with a cut hand."

Heidi put the pictures in her pocket. "You're stupid shed gave my daughter tetanus and I should sue you for that," threatened Heidi.

"No way, you would lose. Your daughter should just keep her hands to herself. And while she's in juvenile hall serving my boyfriend's sentence, I'll see to it that she gets her three full meals a day and some anti-depressant medication."

"Don't be late for the hearing tomorrow," said Amanda. "I know how unpunctual you are, goodbye."

Amanda slammed the door shut and locked it.

When Amanda entered the courtroom the next day with her mother and friend Marie she was sweating. The three of them sat down and waited for the judge to speak. Amanda could see Erin sitting at a table on the other side of the room.

Only about ten minutes went by before the judge came to his seat. "I am Judge Day and I have looked over all of the evidence and facts and have seen the results. I have come to a decision and I have it now." The room was very quiet for a minute and everyone seemed to have their fingers crossed.

"Erin Horn, you are guilty of vandalism and robbery. We will release the suspect, Richard Thompson, and you will serve the sentence he was given. I also want you to give back the furniture you stole from Miss Weaver's shed. You have no chance for a smaller sentence and I want to see you on good behavior for the next year and a half. I am also getting a restraining order against you. You cannot go within a mile of Amanda Weaver or Richard Thompson after you are released. Do you understand?"

Erin nodded her head and responded, "Yes." Two officers placed handcuffs on her.

"In addition to the twelve months that you have just received in the vandalism sentence, I am adding six more months for the furniture that was taken from the shed and for the theft of the car that we found in your garage. That makes a total of eighteen months."

Richard was sitting in front of the judge and had his cuffs taken off as the judge told him he was free to go.

Erin approached Amanda. "It looks like you get your furniture back and your boyfriend. Bye forever. Oh and your shed has the tetanus bacteria." Erin held up her stitched wrist and showed it to Amanda.

Amanda rushed out of the door, running to catch Richard in the parking lot; she hugged him. "I'm so glad you're free. I'll call you."

Amanda had won what she fought for and was not going to give him up.

Chapter 11

Reflections

Amanda was enjoying a lazy summer day when there was a knock at the door. It was a tall police officer. "Your car is out front and we also have the furniture Erin stole. Where should we put the furniture?"

"Just bring it into the living room. We won't be keeping it in the shed anymore."

When the men were finished bringing in the furniture Amanda was glad to see it again. Recognizing her pretty100-year-old wood vanity table with a mirror, she sat down in front of it and stared at her reflection.

The sun set and the sky started to become dark. It was pitch black out by the time Amanda had all of her furniture put away in the attic. It was midnight and she could only hear the scratching of a mouse after her parents had gone to bed.

Amanda sat on an old couch in the attic. She could not sleep and was worried that Richard was going to break up with her. Amanda also felt bad for Erin even though Erin deserved her punishment. That might have been because Erin was sick and serving time in juvenile hall like the criminal that she was.

"Get up!" Amanda heard, and felt a shake. It was Mark. "We have to break down the shed and take it to the junkyard. Go downstairs and eat, then get some gloves, and we'll get started." Waking up on a couch Amanda felt a little sick since she didn't get enough sleep. That night she had fallen asleep in the attic. She went downstairs to look at the clock and it was only 7 a.m. She brushed her hair back into a ponytail and put on a pair of gardening gloves. "Thank God Erin left us the backyard rose bushes."

Amanda walked towards Mark. "How are we going to do this?"

They both pushed the shed towards the front yard. Amanda then took a hose and sprayed the rose bushes with water.

Mark unscrewed all of the screws to take down the walls. They fell and the ceiling fell down. They took the walls and put them in the back of a truck. "We are going down to the junkyard to dump this off. We might as well do it now and get it over with."

With a nod Amanda jumped in to the front seat of the truck. "How far away is the junkyard?"

"About 45 minutes."

"Don't you think we should tell the owner the shed is nasty?" Amanda asked.

"Yes, we will," Mark drove onto the highway. When they arrived at the junkyard, a man at the gate came to Mark's car window.

"What do you have?"

"It's a shed," Mark answered.

"So it's not worth anything?"

"No, it's trouble and we need to get rid of it."

"Okay, bring your truck in and take the shed out." The man opened his gate.

"It's sharp so you want to wear gloves when you handle it." Mark was getting out of the truck.

The man nodded and they placed the shed in a steel dumpster. "It can stay in there and we'll try to melt it down this Wednesday.

I'm Bobby Greenery," the man said as he held out his hand for Mark to shake.

He shook his hand and said, "Thanks for all your help. We've got to get going. We just needed to get rid of that old shed. Amanda, I need to stop at the drugstore for your mother on the way home."

Amanda went into the drugstore and went to the card section. She picked out a get well card for Erin. There was a white, wet, small puppy on the cover and on the inside and it said, *Get well. I hope you feel better then you look.*

As soon as Amanda got home she addressed the card to the girl's juvenile hall where Erin was and then placed it in the mailbox.

At the evening dinner Amanda asked, "Mom, did you know that Erin Horn gets to stay in a pretty cool girls' juvenile hall? I think it's called Atlantic Mistress Correctional Facility."

"Yes and I hope she learns her lesson," Alice replied.

"And I hope she never comes back here. Let's say our prayers before we eat." Amanda had chosen to start with the Serenity prayer. It was one of her favorites. *"God grant me the serenity to accept the things I cannot change, the courage to change the things I can, and the wisdom to know the difference. Thank you God, Amen."*

That prayer would help Amanda relax before trouble began again.

Chapter 12

True Adoration

"Oh Amanda guess what?" Alice greeted Amanda as she came down the hall on a July morning. "We're moving to Hartford, Connecticut. Isn't that exciting? I thought you might like that after all of the trouble you've had here with Erin. You can take your senior year at Hartford High School where it's beautiful and peaceful, and you can concentrate on your homework better. Do you remember how pretty it was there?"

"Yes, there's a good side to this idea and I do feel a little better. But I don't really want to move. This is my home and Marie is my best friend and Richard's my boyfriend," Amanda answered.

"You haven't spoken to that silly boy in two weeks," her mother answered.

"Do we have to move?"

"Yes."

Amanda smiled and turned around. "When?"

"The first week of August so you can start packing whenever you want. Mark has already found us a house."

Amanda nodded and went into her room and collapsed on her bed upset. The thought of moving from Richard Thompson made her upset and she wanted to cry.

She heard the front door shut and her mother and Mark drive away in his car. Amanda ran to the front door and grabbed her mother's car keys. Swiftly driving, fifteen minutes later she was at Richard Thompson's doorstep knocking on his door. When he answered, she hugged him.

"Amanda come in."

"Bad news," Amanda said crying. "I'm moving. We can't graduate together and we can't be together."

"Where to?" Richard asked, looking concerned.

"Hartford, Connecticut, near where we vacationed. Can I stay here with you?"

"I don't know. Are you sure you still want to be with me after what happened?"

"Yes," Amanda answered.

"It's okay. Hartford is not that far away. I'll visit you."

"But we were meant to be and this is going to tear us farther apart. I'll miss you."

"You can stay here."

"I don't have a job. Maybe I could find one in a restaurant. But my mother will never let me stay here. I'll ask her. Maybe we should get married. I still have a whole month."

"You have to be 18. How old are you?" Richard asked.

"I just turned 17, remember, while you were in juvenile hall?"

"I'll have to think about these things."

"Why don't you come home with me tonight and you can meet my mother? We can have dinner and tell her about our plans."

"Okay, I see that you've cheered up," Richard answered.

That night the couple's dreams for a happily ever after began. Amanda was so excited about the idea of being married to him that she started planning her wedding.

Alice was thrilled when she found out Richard was coming to dinner. She and Mark really wanted to meet him.

When Amanda and Richard arrived the table was set. "Mom," Amanda shouted.

Realizing her daughter was home she came out to the living room with Mark. They were introduced to Richard and shook his hand.

Both sides acted very politely. "Dinner will be ready in five minutes," Alice told them. Alice went into the kitchen and Amanda followed her. "I think we like him. I mean, I saw him standing in the courtroom, but now that I have met him I think he's very respectful."

"I'm glad because I think that I love him. I've never had a boyfriend before and now I know what I have been saving myself for."

They sat and Alice placed hot steaming platters of food on the table. They all sat quietly and listened to Alice talk to Richard about Amanda, about when she was a baby and her growing up. Alice obviously liked Richard which was what Amanda had hoped for.

As Alice cut chocolate cake slices for dessert, Amanda decided this was the time to bring up marriage.

"Mom, I'm thinking about staying here with Richard and marrying him. We'd still go to school. How's that sound?"

"No, you're going to Connecticut with us and you can move back here and marry Richard when you're 19," her mother answered.

"That's not so bad," Amanda blew Richard a kiss. "That gives me a year to plan a wedding."

Mark rolled his eyes at the sight. He never thought he would hear her say that.

Holding hands with Richard, Amanda got up from the table and they started to leave.

"Where are you going?" Amanda's mother asked.

"I'm going back to Richard's house with him to get the car." Amanda stood up and kissed her mother on the cheek. "Then we're going to Marie's house for a farewell drink. We won't be gone long," Amanda shut the door. She was in a good mood on the warm starry night, because Richard made her happy. He drove the car with her by his side. She couldn't leave him because her heart told her he was her future.

Chapter 13

Leaving for a Haven

The second week of August Amanda was packed and ready to leave. She had made a farewell dinner date with Richard. "We will go wherever you want," Amanda told Richard.

Richard with all of his taste picked a restaurant that was one hour away in Long Island. During the candlelight dinner, everything seemed perfect. Too perfect for Amanda. "I'm not going to leave. We can go away together, maybe to Massachusetts. I'll get the money I was supposed to be saving to go to a university. Then when I graduate from high school, I'll get a job and earn it back. What do you think?"

"Alright. I'd do anything for you Amanda. My Aunt Ruth lives in Gloucester. We can stay with her. You and I can go to school there." They enjoyed dinner except they received it cool. "Excuse me, waitress. Can you take this back and heat it up please?" Richard asked a passing woman.

"No it's warm enough. I don't have time," she replied.

"Yummy, cold food," Amanda joked. "I think she just doesn't want to admit she made a mistake. Can we go to a motel now? I don't want my mother to find me. What's the plan?"

"Spend the night tonight. I'll call my aunt and pack. If your mother comes to the door, we won't answer it. When she leaves for work tomorrow, we'll go and get your stuff. It's all packed already, isn't it?"

"That's the perfect plan. After we get to Massachusetts, I want to start planning our wedding," Amanda told him. Amanda spent the rest of the night with Richard worrying about her mother.

"Richard, I forgot, I don't have the key to my house."

"How can we get in? Are we going to break in?" he asked.

"I guess."

"Let's go."

"Wait, I want to write my mother a goodbye letter. It's the best I can do for her so she doesn't worry." After writing the letter they both left to take Amanda's belongings.

"I brought a bat to break the window." Richard swung the bat.

"Wait, we don't need it." Amanda jumped over the fence and into the backyard. She opened the gate for Richard. She pointed to the kitchen window that was open.

He pushed out the screen and crawled in. The door opened for Amanda. They loaded up the car with boxes and a suitcase. Amanda placed a letter on the kitchen table and they left.

"Why do I feel like I'll never see my mother again? I'll call her but I won't tell her where I am. Are we going straight to Massachusetts or are we going home first?"

"We need to leave now. Your mother is going to find that note and come looking for us. First I need to get my suitcases." Richard turned on a street that led to his house. "Say goodbye to your old life." They both waved goodbye.

While on the highway, the car stopped. Richard turned the wheel to the right side of the road. "Oh gosh we're out of gas." Richard looked frustrated.

"You airhead! You forgot to get gas."

"You forgot, too," he replied.

"What are we going to do now?" Amanda asked.

"We need to walk to a gas station and get a can of gas. Hopefully there's one nearby. And since you're being so smart today, you can come, too." They locked up the car and started walking towards the first shopping center they saw.

"Where's the nearest gas station?" Richard asked the store clerk whose name tag read Diana.

"Just walk down the street and three blocks away you'll see a gas station."

Richard thanked her and started walking down the block to look for gas.

"Wait, let's get something to drink. It's going to be hot out," Amanda grabbed his arm to stop him.

"You're right."

It only took them one hour to get the can of gas, get the car to the station, and fill it up.

"Let's take the highway that goes along the ocean. It's much more entertaining to look at," Amanda demanded.

Richard did not answer, but turned his car toward the coast highway in agreement. "My aunt expects us there tomorrow morning."

"Richard, stop the car," Amanda demanded.

"Why I thought you said you liked the coast? Open the window for the fresh air."

"My stomach hurts. I'm going to be sick." Amanda took off her seat belt.

"I can't just pull over. Come on, we're only three more hours from the hotel."

"You said we'd only be driving until night time. Pull over!"

Richard took an exit and drove into a parking lot.

Amanda got out of the car and fell over dizzy. She took a big drink of her soda and sat down on the gravel. Bending over holding her stomach she felt sick.

"Did you do this when you were in Hartford?"

"No, I'm not used to driving in your car, sorry," Amanda replied.

"I don't think it rides very smooth." After fifteen minutes Amanda was back in the car. It was late afternoon and she couldn't wait to get there. "I wonder what my mother's doing. I'll bet she's mad."

"She probably is," Richard replied as they passed a cat that lay in the middle of the road stiff from being road kill.

In the morning they pulled up to a beautiful, two-story, blue and white house in a suburb of Gloucester, Massachusetts. The yard only had some patches of grass.

"I could do some nice gardening on this yard here on the corner of Maple Street." Amanda stepped out of the car.

They walked up the sidewalk with Richard holding the suitcases and his hair blowing in the wind. They knocked on the door and Ruth answered.

"Hi." She hugged Richard. "Is this Amanda?"

Amanda nodded her head. And they went inside.

"How do you like it here?" Richard's Aunt Ruth asked.

"It's just as great as it always was. I've been here before."

"We're going to have dinner in an hour and then you need to go to bed. You have school in the morning. And don't think you're sharing the same room. Start getting yourself unpacked."

"Can I call my mother?" Amanda was led to her bedroom phone.

After dinner Amanda met Richard in his bedroom. "Was your mother mad?"

"Yes, she tried to get me to tell her where I was, but I wouldn't. She didn't move like they planned so I feel bad about that. I told her to move. I hope she listens. Now I'm going to start planning our wedding, okay? We can graduate next June, then have the wedding in July. We'll go on our honeymoon to Hawaii."

"With what money?" Richard asked.

"I'll get a job."

"With what time? You'll be in school. I don't think we can afford a big wedding. My aunt can't help us, either."

"This is going to be a cheap wedding then. Maybe we'll get married outside by the beach. Goodnight, I love you." Amanda shut the door behind her not letting the lack of finances drag her mood down to sorrow.

Chapter 14

Wedding Wishes

May of 1971 came quickly and Amanda was excited about graduating and her upcoming wedding. So excited, she called her mother. She did not tell her about the wedding though. "I'm getting good grades," she told her mother.

Her mother did move to Connecticut like she wanted. Amanda realized she was now closer to her. "Don't worry Mom I'm great." Amanda and Richard did not see Erin Horn before they left. She was still locked up. They didn't care if they ever saw her again.

The wedding day came too slowly for Amanda. She had planned to get married on the local beach. That was all they could afford.

There wouldn't be a formal reception, either. The point was for her to get married and that was all. Between the two of them they came up with enough money for the license and maybe some champagne.

Waking up early in the morning, the room seemed dark. When she looked out of the curtains the sky was gray and cloudy. The window felt cold. Walking into the living room the fireplace was lit. Richard was sitting on the couch. There was a knock at the door.

Amanda peeked and almost fainted at the sight of the visitor. Richard dragged her out of the way and opened the door. It was Amanda's mother. She was holding a gift wrapped in white and silver. She didn't look angry actually but was smiling.

"What a surprise. we didn't expect you."

"I came to see Amanda's wedding." Alice handed him a gift. Amanda sat up.

"How did you find us?" Richard asked.

"I got caller ID and then traced the phone number to this area. Then I looked you up in the phone book. I can't believe you didn't send me an invitation! And I missed your graduation! I've missed Amanda so much. When is the wedding?"

"It's at one. On Gloucester beach," answered Richard. "Actually there isn't much of a wedding."

"Come in," Amanda said. "I'm sorry about everything. You know how impatient I get. Please come to our little wedding. Go get your suitcase and stay here with us. How long will you be in town?"

"Just for the weekend. I have to go now. I'll see you at the beach." Alice left quickly.

Amanda sat quietly until she heard the sound of sprinkles hit the roof. Looking out of the window, she saw it was raining. "Oh great! What now? Let's open my mother's present." It was a white toaster oven. Amanda liked it because she always wanted one.

Amanda had kept her dress hidden. Keeping it simple like the wedding. She did not want to be seen dragging a ten-foot long silk, pearl, diamond wedding gown down the sidewalk. She thought fancy dresses like that were for churches and rich families. Hers was locked away in a chest kept away secretly from Richard. It was a simple white lace dress. The dress was a secret for good luck. The idea of having a fancy wedding was only a dream. The dress never left the chest until the day to get married came.

Afterwards the couple would meet Amanda's mother on the beach. After visiting at the beach, they would have lunch. Amanda stood on the beach in her white lace dress. After finishing her vows to Richard, with her veil over her face it was his turn.

To everyone's surprise Richard had written his vows into a marriage poem. *My Darling, you were gentle with my fragile heart, and I've wanted to marry you from the start. My love will always be like new. So now I say I do. I promise I'll always be with you. Please be my wife for all of my life.*" He lifted her veil off of her face then kissed her. He heard everyone clap.

The only reception they would have was a cheeseburger lunch with Alice on the beach. They ate still in their wedding clothes. At the fast food restaurant, Amanda held her mom's suitcase. She was staying with her for the next two nights. Amanda was a little nervous because it was her day to be married and she had just turned eighteen.

Richard announced, "Guess what, Amanda? We are moving to West Virginia. You can go to college there."

"Wow another move!" Amanda didn't want to say anything that would get her into trouble. All that came out was, "Great I can't wait." The idea of having a husband was so exciting. She felt like a super housewife or Lucy from the TV show *I Love Lucy*. Though she did notice that Richard didn't ask her if she wanted to move, Amanda kept quiet.

Amanda spent the rest of the night with her mother. It was goodbye without actually saying that at all. She would be living in West Virginia by September. "Since we don't own any furniture there's nothing to pack." She hugged her mother and then she was gone. For the next month she felt like moving was the only thing that mattered in life.

The move to West Virginia made Amanda Weaver feel great hope. Little did the newlyweds know the gray clouds that floated in the sky indicated their stormy future.

Chapter 15

Morgan's Beginning

February 25, 1945, Tom and Helen Garrison lay next to each other in bed. After a night of romance they relaxed. It was quiet there because they did not live in a crowded neighborhood. Their house was by itself down a dirt road called Mud Lane in the Parkersburg, West Virginia, town. Even their three-month-old daughter, Morgan, lay asleep in her crib not making a sound.

Helen heard a bang of thunder and knew it was a storm. She did not mind it, though. Getting up out of bed she put on her tan robe.

Standing in the kitchen she heard rain begin to pound on the windows. The sound was soothing. It made her feel peaceful, sleepy, and in love.

The house was dark. Walking upstairs to the baby's room she checked to see if everything was okay and shut the door. Lying down on her blue couch she fell asleep.

It rained the next day all day. Looking outside, Helen saw it was gray, cold, and misty. Her husband came home for lunch and she cooked for him and fed baby Morgan. This was all. She did not have a job yet. Not after just having a baby. Helen wouldn't start working for another two years.

Evening came and the sky darkened. Helen wanted to have dinner ready for her husband. It was still cold and raining so she built a fire in the fireplace. She stepped into the kitchen and couldn't see so she flipped the light switch. Nothing happened, no light. Running around she tried every switch she could find. The power was out. It must have been out in the whole town.

Helen still wanted to cook dinner so she lit a white candle and went to work on spaghetti. There was a tree in her front yard that was covering one of the windows. When there was light it created many shadows that gave Helen shivers. Looking over at Morgan she knew the baby was too little to be afraid of the dark. This tree was so big it was taller than her two-story home.

The house was made mostly of bricks. It was twenty years old. White curtains hung on every window and the carpet was tan. That night it was surrounded by puddles. Helen knew her husband would be home in an hour.

He would decide what to do about the electricity. The front door slammed. It was Tom Garrison. His first action was to flip the light switch. Nothing happened and he noticed the house was completely dark. Walking into the kitchen he saw his wife. "I'll call the electric company and have them send someone out to work on it."

Candles were lit all over the house. Quiet shadows were cast everywhere. "He'll be here in thirty minutes," Tom told his wife.

The rain started again and the house got darker with every minute. Looking out the window Helen could see a strong wind blowing the house-sized tree. Being strong, it stood tall.

Headlights hit the windows and light entered the house. The couple sat up and knew the electrician had arrived. Helen ran upstairs and picked up the baby. She waited for her husband to answer the door.

Opening the door Tom saw a short man with hardly any hair. He walked up the sidewalk and held out his hand. "I'm Don Mare, the electrician."

They shook hands. The rain had let off, but there were still puddles surrounding the house.

"We have a problem with our outlet box. You need to take a look at it."

"That's what I came here for. Where is it?" asked Don.

"It's in the backyard near the shed. You'll be able to find it."

Don nodded, picked up his tool box, and headed for the backyard. Tom followed behind him and opened the back gate door. The outlet box was surrounded by a puddle of water. Don was upset at the thought of getting his shoes wet. "I can see that the door is open so whoever left it open let the wires get wet." Don walked into the water and saw that the wires were sticking out of the insulation. One wire was wet and another was in half. "I think maybe an animal was chewing through this one. I have some replacement wires. It will only take me an hour."

"Good," Tom Garrison said as he turned around and walked back to the house. Looking up at the night sky it was still cloudy. There was a rumble of thunder that warned of more wet storms.

Tom had gone inside. The area was dark. There wasn't any porch light. Don went to his car and brought out a lantern. There was no rain now only a cold breeze. He yanked out the wire that had broken in half. It was so long he wound it up and put it on top of the box.

While drying off the wet rain that had soaked the inside of the box, Don slipped on a rock in the puddle he was standing in. His arm knocked into the box as he fell. Covered in water the rolled up wire fell in the puddle and sent electricity shocks throughout it. Smoke rose from the water as Don struggled to crawl from the puddle unable to move.

As he was passing out from the shock to his head it was clear to him that Tom had not shut off the electricity switches to the house. They were on and had just started to work as he had dried off the box. Lights flashed through the brick houses windows for a second and there was a calm silence.

In the Garrison house it was midnight and baby Morgan was asleep. "What do you think is taking him so long?" asked Helen.

"I don't know. Go to bed and I'll go and get him in a few minutes. At least the lights are working. His car is outside so he didn't leave," answered Tom. As Tom went outside he shivered in the cold. He gasped and panicked at what he saw. Don lay face down in the puddle of water by the electric box. A wire hung from the box to the puddle.

Tom ran over to him to check his pulse. There was no pulse. Don was dead and tears came to Tom's eyes. His body filled with fear.

He was afraid the police would accuse him of somehow having something to do with Don's death. He panicked and became afraid.

He grabbed a large garbage bag and put Don inside. Placing it in the trunk he drove out ten miles to a field near a cemetery to bury Don.

He did feel guilty, mean, and selfish but the idea of sitting in prison for the rest of his life frightened him. He upset himself by these thoughts and slipped in some mud landing his head on the fresh grave mound.

When he came through the front door of his home it was midnight.

"Where were you?" Helen asked. "What did you do, roll in the mud?"

"Don had an accident with the electricity and was killed. I had to hide his body out in the field down the road, ten minutes away. Try not to worry yourself. In the morning I'll take his car and park it back at his house. Then no one will notice anything's wrong. You just have to promise me that in a few years you will never tell Morgan about this."

"Alright I'll never tell," Helen went into her bedroom and shut the door. At that moment being faithful was all that mattered to her, but she was not the best at keeping secrets.

Chapter 16

The Arrival

September 2, 1971. Amanda Thompson rode excitedly with her husband Richard up their new driveway. Their house in Parkersburg, West Virginia, was fifty years old, but all Richard could afford. Amanda liked it and thought it was cute. "The bricks are what make the house so strong." It was the old Morgan house.

"I love Parkersburg. It's so cozy. A lot of Civil War soldiers were from Parkersburg. That's so exciting. People say the soldiers haunt local fields and old factories, but I don't believe the stories. Aren't you excited? Maybe we could plan to have a child. There's enough room in this house." Richard was a little stiff and tired from the drive and didn't answer.

"I'm going to check out the town now," she said.

"No you're not. You're going to help me unpack first. At least some of this stuff," Richard demanded as he opened the front door to the house. His new job was at the local carpet shop where he would sell carpet until he graduated from college with a degree in medicine.

"I'll go as soon as we unload the truck and get everything in here." Stepping in the doorway she ran through the two-level house checking out every room. She ran all the way to the attic. The door squeaked open. It was dusty with spider webs. At least she thought it would be a place to store the stuff they didn't need.

It had taken four hours for them to unload the moving truck. While Richard was gone returning their borrowed truck and the sun was setting. Stars started to appear as Amanda drove away in Richard's car that he had towed to their new residence.

Driving around she was pleased with what she saw. The neighborhoods were nice and clean. The malls were not too far in shopping distance. The lights were on at the church, Parkersburg Assembly, so Amanda decided to go in.

The first face she saw was that of beautiful Morgan Garrison. Her name tag also read Assistant Pastor. Her eyes were light hazel and she had few specks of brown freckles on her checks that must have been placed there when the good Lord created her. Her wavy dark brown hair hung past her shoulders and lay on her desk as she read a upcoming activity announcement.

"Hi, what time does church start?" Amanda asked.

"On Saturday night at seven and three times on Sunday morning. Here, let me give you the list. If you're new here then I have a fill out sheet for your facts. Here's my card in case you need to call me." Amanda filled out the personal information card and gave it back to Morgan. "I'll be in church this Saturday night. Will you be there?"

"Yes, I also teach Monday night ladies bible study. It's only one night a month. You might like to attend that. Are you new to this area? I don't think I've seen you before."

"I just moved here today from New York. I got married a couple of months ago so my husband's here too. I'm looking for a part-time job while I go to college. Do you need any help?"

"Yes, but first you need to take classes here at the church. I teach some of those, too. There are only about eight. You're welcome to show up." Morgan held out her hand for Amanda to shake

"I'll be there," Amanda shook her hand. "Are you originally from Parkersburg?"

"Yes I was born and raised here," Morgan answered. "See you Saturday, bye."

Amanda liked the city she was in. Its old-fashion look appealed to her. It seemed so friendly. When she left the church it was dark.

The wind started to blow and made a whistling sound. She hurried back to her car. Driving back home, she passed the old town cemetery called Riverview. Ten minutes later she was home.

"I think I've seen most of this town now. Tomorrow I might want to see the Ohio River," Richard only glanced back as he unpacked a box.

One hour later there was a knock at the door. It was Morgan Garrison. "I just wanted to bring you these flowers and a bible. This is the church's welcoming gift to you. I can't wait to see you in my class this Monday."

"Come in. So this is a really old town?"

"Yes, I live fifteen minutes from here with my roommate, Kate. We rent an apartment. Rent is always so hard to make. I haven't finished my college education yet. I'm just a training pastor. I don't live with my mother because I can't stand it in her old house. I grew up here so I know this town is mysterious. Cute but not always peaceful. If I was rich, I'd probably move away."

"My mother, Helen, lives over on Juliana Street. I hate to have to ask her for financial help so my roommate and I are like sisters.

Maybe you'll meet my mother some time. My father died ten years ago. He's buried in Riverview. Can't say I miss him much. When I was ten he locked me in our basement for punishment. I still can't forgive him. It was creepy. Rain was pouring down. The walls creaked and I found a dead rat. He did not let me out until my mother made him in the morning. I couldn't see anything down there except one flash of light that lingered around the door. That house is haunted.

I think that if we figured out why it would stop. A lot of houses in this town are haunted. You're not afraid of ghosts, are you, Amanda?"

Amanda shook her head no.

I'll bet my father is one now. A darn big one. Morgan drank the hot chocolate that Amanda poured her. "I hope you're prepared for some cold. It gets much stormier. Thank you, but I have to leave now." Morgan disappeared out the door.

Amanda turned and hugged Richard. "Let's have a picnic by the Ohio River tomorrow," Richard suggested.

By midnight they had laid a mattress down to sleep on. The wood floors creaked from the wind. "How can a brick house screech?" Amanda asked. There was a knock at the door.

Richard left to answer it then came back. "There was no one there."

"How could there not be anyone there?"

"Maybe I took too long and they ran away. You know how kids are."

In the morning they both drove by the Ohio River to take a look. They sat down beside the bank and drank orange juice. "I wonder if I could fish in there." Richard stared into the water.

"Will you give me a ride to the church? I want to go to the bible study classes."

Richard agreed and they both left. He dropped her off at the church and watched her walk away into one of the rooms.

It was past time for the class to start and Amanda sat there waiting with everyone else. There were newsletters that explained the classes and she took the time to read them. She could tell that people were wandering in and out looking for the teacher. The teacher was Miss Garrison. That's what it said on the sign up sheet.

Morgan did not show up which was a disappointment to Amanda. She really admired Morgan. Not just because she was pretty, but because of her leadership qualities. A lady who worked in the office named Kathy substituted for Morgan. Morgan couldn't make it.

Amanda liked the class and the church. Kathy called Morgan on the phone to find out the problem.

Morgan said her mother borrowed her car. She was supposed to return it in time for her class, but didn't. Morgan didn't know when she would be returning to work she had no money for a cab and the church was too far to walk. Her mother was not answering her phone calls.

"I'll be in this Saturday," Morgan told her manager, Steve Grose, on the phone. It had taken several days for Morgan to get her car back. Morgan had lovingly forgiven her mother because she knew her mother loved her. But Kate and Morgan had their rent due and Morgan needed to get back to work so that she could pay her share.

Morgan went into the office to get prepared for her class. She truly loved her job and sat down at her desk and saw Steve passing by.

"Hi Steve. How are you?" Morgan asked.

"Oh I'm fine." He walked in to her office. "I'm going to have to let you go. Everything was running so smoothly when you weren't here and Kathy took over your job. We have too many employees. We need to reduce our payroll."

"You're letting me go? Right now?" Morgan asked.

"This is your last day. Finish today and pick up your final check." Steve went out the door and he was gone.

Morgan was so upset she couldn't concentrate on her work. She worried about ever finding a new job. How was she going to help Kate pay the rent? Tears came to her eyes. She felt like the world was unfair to her.

When the phone rang and she answered it her voice was weak and it shook. It was obvious she was upset. When the tears started to fall that was it. She grabbed her purse and left. They wouldn't have anyone to teach that night's class and she knew that looked bad.

Morgan didn't care because she wasn't coming back anyway. When Morgan got home she made the announcement to Kate. They would decide together what to do next.

"We have to get our rent somewhere or we'll get evicted," Kate told Morgan. "I called your mother and asked for help. She sounded upset to hear about our problem. She said she couldn't offer you any money. You can live with her, though. She said she wanted to help you since you're getting fired was partly her fault. She was so sorry."

"I am going to call her right now. I'm going to try to find another job before I run out of money. I hate to have to move back in with her into her creepy old house."

When October came Morgan started packing. She didn't want to leave, but her job search was unsuccessful. Poor Morgan actually dreaded moving back into that old house on Juliana Street she lived in as a baby. "As soon as I get there I'll find a job as soon as I can. Then I'm right back here. I won't even move all of my things," Morgan told Kate. Morgan moved into her mother's old house.

"I'm glad you're back here." Morgan's mother Helen looked relieved. "I worry about you."

"How is this old haunt?" Morgan was referring to her old brick two-story house.

"It's great. It's cozy and you'll like staying here again. Just go back to your old room." Morgan walked upstairs to her old bedroom on the right. She saw her old dolls and games from when she was a child.

It was dusty and Morgan knew she would be spending the next day cleaning it. All the toys were going into a box and into the attic. It was already dark outside. Her bedroom window was open and a light breeze blew the lacy white curtains. It was still warm out. The cool fall air had not yet come.

Morgan found her framed poem she had written about her faith in God. It read: *God, you comfort my pain. You are my gain. With you no sadness will remain. Lead me on a path to heaven, Where the green grass is made of emerald jewels, in the winter the snowflakes are silver, In the autumn the leaves turn to gold.*

After hanging her poem on her wall she went downstairs to see her mother again. "I love this house again as much as a person can. Mother, are you afraid sometimes?"

"I'm not really afraid. This house isn't as disturbed as it used to be. It got really quiet when your father died. Only the lights flicker on and off sometimes. Only for seconds at a time."

"I brought you a present." Morgan showed her a small box wrapped in pink paper. "It's a nightlight. Put it wherever you want. Probably in the darkest places in the house, like by the stairs. I brought some blessed purple, white, and orange candles. They protect you from evil spirits when lit. Also I brought a crucifix to put on the wall, a dream catcher to suck out bad dreams, and a gourd that's used as a candle-holder. That should make you feel safe."

"What's a crucifix?" Helen asked.

"It's a cross that symbols the execution of Jesus Christ."

"Oh, yes of course."

"I have to go to work in the morning so you have the house all to yourself tomorrow." Helen picked up her nightlight and went to her bedroom.

Morgan went back to her room with hot chocolate and a sleeping pill to help her relax. She plugged in her nightlight, turned it on, and lay down. The last thing she did was close the window. It was open and that bothered her. A bright light downstairs began flashing on and off. She ran downstairs to turn off the kitchen light and when she came back she was shocked. The window was open again. "The wind must have blown it open." She closed it. Before going to sleep the crucifix was nailed on the wall.

Morgan woke to the sound of footsteps coming from the other side of the house. She opened the curtains and a warm light shone on her face. "Mom!" Morgan went into her mother's bedroom. No one was there. "What did you have for breakfast?" She walked downstairs but couldn't find her there either. She was alone.

Since her mother wasn't home Morgan decided to go shopping. She didn't have her car so she didn't buy much. She had also stocked up on small Halloween decorations and bought a small pumpkin to carve into a jack-o-lantern because there was a story that it keeps away ghosts. Her favorites were the orange outside lights.

Before decorating she grabbed a cloth and can of wax to dust her bedroom. "I can't believe she left this room so dirty. I don't think Mother's cleaned it in some time. I think she actually waited for me to come back home and clean it." The doorbell rang, it was Kate.

"Hi, I'm glad you're here. Come in," Morgan opened the door for Kate. They both sat down on the couch. "What are you going to be for Halloween?" Morgan asked.

"I think a fairy."

"I'll be a ghost," Morgan said. They both laughed.

"We'll go to a party this time for sure."

They heard a loud bang come from the attic. It sounded like something had fallen. They both looked up.

"I'm so tired of wondering if this house is haunted. It seems like it's all I think of. I need to know for sure. I'm going to look through the directory and find a psychic. I'll have them come over. They can tell me if the house is haunted. They really aren't expensive. The leaves on the trees are turning brown now. It's kind of sad," Morgan was looking out the window. "The temperature is dropping fast. I wonder if the air conditioner is still on automatic." When Morgan checked, it wasn't.

Morgan's search for a psychic medium was a success. The woman was willing and excited about coming over for an investigation. Her name was Nancy. She came to the Garrison house that night and was led through each room in the house. Her light brown eyes glanced around the rooms. She closed her eyes and bowed her head. Her long brown hair fell over her face.

"Please don't be upset, but I do sense a presence here. I think it's a man. I'll try to make spirit communication. We need to find out who the ghost is and what he wants. He must be attached to the house and the both of you. He haunts for a purpose and I don't know what it is yet. I want you to call me whenever you need me or you think there's activity happening. Your house is haunted. I am going to leave early tonight because it is quiet," Nancy informed Morgan and Helen.

A cloud of smoke passed them by. "Do you have a fireplace?" Nancy asked.

"Yes, but I didn't light it." Helen went to the large gray living room and found a fire in the fireplace. Dark smoke floated around the room.

She opened the chimney vent and a window so the smoke would go away. "Morgan did you light a fire?"

"No, I was with you all afternoon."

"That could have been a spirit. I'll be back tomorrow night with a camera. I don't know if we can get rid of the ghost yet. That can be very hard. You may end up having to move to another town and start over. This town is rumored to be very haunted. You wouldn't be the first to report a disturbance, and it's October, the most haunted month of the year. Be as prepared as you can. As soon as I figure out who the ghost is we'll go to his grave. That way we can be sure he stops haunting you," Nancy told them.

"What are we supposed to do while you're gone?" asked Morgan.

"Don't worry. I sense that you will be okay for tonight. But you must consider moving far from this town. Ghosts haunt a particular area. They stay with the area. If you've lived here all your life, don't you want a change?" Nancy asked.

"Isn't there some kind of a ghost trap? Maybe a ghost spray to keep them out?" Morgan asked.

"Yes, there might be. For now, we will work on what the ghost wants. I'll leave a tape recorder on all night to see what activity we can record." Nancy handed them a tape recorder with a blank tape.

"Press record just before you go to bed." There was a knock at the door. Morgan answered it but there was no one there.

"Don't try to sleep with the lights on tonight. Usually when ghosts know you're recording them they don't make a sound," Nancy told them. "You can keep a nightlight on and that will help keep the haunting activity down."

As Nancy was escorted out the door the phone rang. "Promise me you won't be afraid. Stay in the house at night. Don't open the door for anyone." Nancy waved goodbye and went to her car.

Helen sat on the couch staring at the wall. No one was on the phone. It was a common thing but it gave Helen the shivers. It made her feel like someone was spying on her.

Chapter 17

Twilight Mist

Morgan woke at 1 a.m. To the sound of scratching on a wall. She thought it could be a mouse so she went into the kitchen to grab some mouse traps and cheese for bait. The sound was coming from the guest room. She tiptoed to the closet to set the traps. She also put one under the bed being careful not to make any sound that would wake her mother.

After coming out from under the bed she felt someone tapping on her back. She turned around and didn't see anyone. Morgan tried to get up to turn the light on, but there was a heavy whack on the back of her head. She fell unconscious

When Morgan awoke she was in a tomb at Riverview cemetery. The sight of a dark figure floated around the corner. It turned around and she saw its face was a ghostly skull. Morgan thought that it must have been the person who hit her. Feeling the back of her head there was only a bump. She breathed a sigh of relief and sat up. The tomb door shut. Reaching for the door Morgan's hands shook. She pressed on it with all her strength. It would not budge. Morgan had her head in her lap thinking she was trapped and convinced that the person that attacked her was a ghost.

The only thought that comforted her at the time was that her mother would wake in the morning and find her gone. Her mother would be looking for her. A cement box lay in the center of the tomb. Wanting to look in it Morgan began pushing the top off. *I hope no one's in there.* The cement top slammed to the floor. *Oh great.* The decomposed body of a man was as still and lifeless as a doll. This really darkened Morgan's situation. It had a terrible odor. She couldn't wait to leave because the place smelled like burned hair and garbage. She placed the top of the lid back on the coffin.

Morgan sat next to the door. Patiently she hoped to find a single ray of light when the morning came if the tomb would let any rays in. She couldn't wait for the morning. Thank God for the crack of dawn.

Just as Morgan predicted, her mother was looking for her. After a long day at work, when it was dark out again, Helen called the police to report the disappearance. "I try not to worry. I know she's okay. It's probably some emergency at her friend's house or something. She could be partying or shopping at the mall, not even remembering to call her mother. I called all of her friends to see if they had seen her. Kate wasn't home. I did get Amanda Thompson. She said she'd stop by tomorrow morning and help me look for Morgan," Helen told the officer when he came to the door. They were optimistic about Morgan's situation.

At the next sunset Amanda Thompson felt upset. As time passed, the sadder she became and she didn't really know why. "It's getting dark. I need to go to Mrs. Garrison's house like I promised," Amanda told Richard. "When all this is over I'm going on vacation." Her idea for a vacation was Blennerhassett Island. It was close to Parkersburg, West Virginia. It was pretty, peaceful, and old-fashioned.

It would be perfect for her and Richard. She was feeling excited and instead of going straight to the Garrisons she went to buy a ticket to ride a boat to the island and made hotel reservations.

Arriving at the port where the boat leaves she sat in the grass and relaxed. The sight was breathtaking to her. It was green and the water was a clear warm bluish-green. The sight made her smile. It was worth every penny. She could even see tiny white and yellow wild flowers around the edges of the Blennerhassett Lake.

After buying a ticket it became dark. The moon was now in company with the stars. It was quiet because no one was around.

There were quiet splashes and Amanda realized it was the fish in the lake that were jumping. Looking into the water she saw her reflection.

For once Amanda had forgotten she was worried about Morgan. The autumn air was still warm. She stood up and took off her jeans and off came her shirt. She walked up to the shore and stepped in.

The water was cool and it felt good. She let her whole body fall into the water and began swimming.

She swam out to some broken branches that were floating on the water. Weeds from the bottom of the water were brushing on her feet. Mysteriously a dark shadow came over the water. Green branches from the bottom reached up like a hand, wrapped around her ankle, and pulled her under the water!

Amanda went straight down. The branches were pulling her under. Almost hitting the bottom she grabbed them and tore them off of her. Splashing up through the surface she quickly swam to the shore and started running as fast as she could to her car. She picked up her clothes and put them on but was still gasping for her breath.

As Amanda ran she looked back to see if someone or something was following her. Running into something she thought was a tree, she turned around. It was a girl ghost in a brown dress. She had long brown hair and appeared to be about 10 years old.

"Excuse me," Amanda said. "I wasn't looking where I was going."

"Are you in a hurry?" the girl asked.

"I guess. So I'd better go. Try and stay away from that lake. It could be dangerous."

"I don't worry much these days. I'm not really afraid of anything."

"It's getting late. Isn't your mother looking for you?" asked Amanda.

"No I don't have a mother any more. I guess you could say I was an orphan. You'd better get going. And why don't you be careful."

"Yes, I'll see you around." Amanda ran to her car door and jumped in. Looking back to the place she just came from she didn't see the girl. She pulled her hair up into a bun and drove towards Morgan's house.

Fifteen minutes later Amanda was knocking on Morgan's door.

"I'm sorry I'm late," she told Helen. "Is Morgan back yet?"

"No," Helen shook her head from side to side. "I'm going to buy a big dog tomorrow. There are good reasons for that. I'll feel safe and I'm taking him on a search for Morgan. Why don't you spend the night? You can sleep in the guest room. Tomorrow I'll get up early and shop for a dog. When I get home we can go out looking for Morgan."

"Okay," Amanda agreed. She wandered around the house looking because she really liked what she saw. She thought Helen was very nice to her. Immediately she called Richard on her cell phone to tell him where she was and that she was spending the night there.

When Amanda woke it was early afternoon. She had already slept too late. Looking around the house she saw that Helen wasn't home yet. While eating a bagel and some pineapple for breakfast she waited for her to come home with a dog.

When Helen came through the door she said, "I hope Morgan is happily surprised when she comes home and sees the dog. I think it's a German Shepherd. I haven't thought of a name for him yet." He was a big, long haired, black animal with patches of brown. It was not a puppy. Luckily for Helen he did like to sniff a lot.

"Why don't you call him Shaggy?" Amanda asked.

"That's a good idea, we'll call him Shaggy."

"Do you prefer to be called Helen, Mrs. Garrison, or Mom?"

"Just call me Helen. When you're ready we are going to look for Morgan," answered Helen.

"I'm ready, just a second."

Standing outside Helen had the dog on a leash. "We are going to look everywhere."

Helen watched the dog sniff the ground. "We are going to let him lead the way. Morgan's probably hiding from us somewhere." The dog started sniffing towards the park. They followed him wherever he went. Sometimes they laughed because he almost led them out into the woods.

"Morgan! Alright she doesn't hear us. Let's go in another direction," said Amanda.

They were still walking with the dog when finally they saw Riverview Cemetery. "I think he's tracking other people instead. We should have let him sniff one of Morgan's shoes to be sure he knows who he's looking for," Amanda said.

The sun started to set and they both started to get upset that Morgan had not come home. Fog started coming in as they both followed the dog into the graveyard. He started running and Helen dropped the leash. She could hear the dog barking loudly. "Shaggy," Helen called as they both caught up with him.

"Great," said Amanda, because she saw Shaggy digging at someone's gravestone. Next the dog was jumping on top of a tombstone that was leaned up against someone's tomb. He was barking loudly.

Both ladies pushed the large stone away and off of the tomb door. Shaggy continued to growl at the tomb door. They were afraid to pull her away. The dog kept scratching at the door. It moved open a little.

When Helen looked in she screamed when she saw Morgan. Morgan was lying on the cement, unconscious. Helen ran over and saw that Morgan was still alive. She hugged and kissed her daughter, thanking God that she had found her.

"Amanda will you help me lift her? We need to carry her home and then take her to the hospital."

Amanda and Helen carried Morgan home as quickly as they could. They were almost running with Shaggy chained to Amanda's arm. When they got home Helen placed Morgan in her car.

Later that night while Amanda was resting, Helen came in the guest room. "Morgan is going to be okay. She was dehydrated and can come home tomorrow. She's awake now. Everyone is calling her problem an accident at the hospital. Morgan seemed upset about this. Why would she break into a tomb? She claims someone did this to her, but doesn't know who and she seemed delirious, not making any sense. I'll talk to her about it when she comes home." Helen left the room.

As Amanda lay on the bed she watched the window eerily slide open. A cold wind blew into the room and paper blew everywhere. Autumn leaves blew in and made the room a mess. She shut the window and ran downstairs.

"Let's make a welcoming dinner for her tomorrow. It will cheer her up. We'll have chicken, mashed potatoes and gravy, rolls, and cake. I'll do the cooking and we can light candles," Amanda said.

The idea was agreed upon. "I know Morgan is going to want us to move and I don't know what to do," Helen said.

"Halloween is next week. I'll take her to a party and she'll forget about it for a while." Amanda smiled at Helen knowing this was a good idea.

When Morgan came home they were all excited. They all had a very enjoyable dinner together. Morgan told her mother that it was a ghost that kidnapped her and put her in the tomb. Her mother believed her because she knew the house was haunted. "I think we'll consider moving now," Helen said. She had lived there many years.

"I think that would be a good idea. I can find a job working in another church in another state, maybe in Illinois. I don't know how I can stand another night here. I hope that ghost is gone. As long as there are no more ghosties, I'm fine."

When night fell the house became cold. "I'll start a fire," Morgan said. Amanda left to go home and it was just Morgan, her mother, and the dog Shaggy outside. Morgan sat by the fire in her thick white sweater trying to warm up. Wind started to whistle and the giant sized tree began scratching on the window. It started to sound like a human scratching. Small drizzles of rain drops hit the window with tapping.

"It's raining. Go out back and get the dog. We will bring him in for tonight," said Helen.

Morgan went to the dog. It was raining hard and night had fallen. She grabbed Shaggy by the collar and tried to bring him to the front yard to get his leash. When she unlocked the gate she lost hold of the dog and he started running all around the yard. Then he ran down the street that was lit up by a sudden flash of lightening. Morgan heard the gate squeak loudly. Her hair blew in the wind and was soaking wet as she shut the gate.

When Morgan approached her mother she was soaked. "The dog ran away."

"Alright that's okay. We'll go look for him in the car."

"Wait. I'm soaking wet. Let me change first."

"By the time you're done he might be in Ohio, hurry. Doesn't the dog make you feel safe?" The lights went out and they heard the sound of thunder rumbling. Blue lightning lit up the house.

The lights came back on and Morgan had her jacket on with her wet hair pulled back in a ponytail. "Yes, I'm ready." Morgan grabbed an umbrella and they went to the car.

"Do you have the leash?" Helen asked.

"Yes."

They drove around town for a while in the dark pouring rain.

"We're never going to find him. Look there." Morgan could see the dog's paw prints. They grabbed a flashlight and an umbrella and started following the tracks. It wasn't long before they found Shaggy. He was digging in the mud.

"Here Shaggy. Come on," they called.

Morgan approached the dog alone when she saw its silhouette in the dark. "I'm over here!"

When Helen heard her call she went running after her. Halfway there she slipped and fell in the mud but was unharmed and quickly got up to go to Morgan. The dog was scratching and chewing on a plastic bag. The dog ripped it open and Morgan screamed when seeing the corpse of a dead man's body revealed. It was badly decomposed, a skeleton with a face.

"What are we going to do now?" Morgan asked.

"We could take it to the police or the morgue."

"No we can't. We'll have to leave it here and call the police to come and investigate. Now let's get out of here," Morgan said as she walked towards the car in the rain.

"Wait," her mother said, as she ran with the leash to get Shaggy.

When they arrived home Helen called the local police station and gave them the location of the body.

"We will need to talk to you and your friend," the sergeant said.

"Give me your phone number and address and we will be in touch." Helen gave him the information and hung up the phone relieved the day was over.

The next few weeks in the house were peaceful. There wasn't a single disturbance. Helen still wanted to sell the house and move to Ohio. Just before they left and everything in the old house was boxed up the police called. Helen was informed the body they found was Don Mare, a local electrician who had disappeared long ago. She was silent with shock and remembered he was the man who had come to fix their electrical problem so many years ago and what her late husband told her he had done. At that moment, she became angry with him and just wanted to leave the room to be alone.

Don's body was laid to rest in the local graveyard and the Garrison house was never haunted again. Morgan never heard the truth about how Don had died in their yard. She didn't know the real reason the house had been disturbed. She was just glad to be moving far away from the old place.

Amanda and Richard Thompson stopped by to see them off. "We really haven't seen any haunting disturbances around town," Amanda told Morgan. "But I think I've seen a little orphan girl in a brown dress wondering around the children's playground at night. I think she has a birthmark on her right arm.

"There she is right there," Amanda pointed to a photo of some children Helen had sitting on top of a box.

"That can't be her. That's a picture of my husband when he was a child. The girl standing next to him was a school mate of his. She died in a car accident when she was ten years old"

"I'm sure that was her," Amanda answered.

"We did hear that a few people claim they've seen her wandering around the park, but who knows," said Helen.

They were not sad, but were smiling, knowing that they would all see each other again by keeping in touch. Amanda and Morgan had become the confident people they had always wanted to be and would have everything they ever wanted in life.

An Affair In Bloom

Chapter 1

The Awakening

Molly Dew felt the heat of the morning summer sun burn her flesh while she still tried to sleep. Waking up Monday morning to the sound of her husband Andy breaking dishes, but not understanding why, Molly wandered into the kitchen and asked, "What are you doing?"

You didn't load the dishwasher last night! All the dishes are dirty and now I don't have any clean plates for my breakfast." He pulled a dish out of the sink and threw it up against the wall, breaking it. "I'm sick of you being an independent, lazy, broad. Like you think you don't have to do anything just because you have a kid." He grabbed Molly by her hair and lifted her head up because she was looking at the ground. He made a fist and hit her in the mouth. His face turned red and he said, "I'll eat out this morning. While you're sitting around, why don't you start taking lessons on how to be a good wife." He slammed the door behind him and left for work.

Molly began loading the dishwasher and then swept up the broken dishes. Her little Angela was still asleep so she called the babysitter to come watch her seven year old daughter while she went to look for good wife lessons. At least that's what Molly told the babysitter.

Really deep in her heart she wanted to get revenge against the husband who gave her a fat lip. He had been violent like that before.

When the babysitter arrived she was ready to leave and go anywhere. Maybe to the local college to look for interesting classes, or to collect job applications. Maybe even buy a shot gun to get rid of the husband she felt didn't respect her. No Molly would never do that ever. Her revenge would be good and productive.

While sitting in a restaurant waiting for the waitress to serve her lunch she couldn't figure out exactly what she wanted to do. But she was sorry and afraid of Andy and knew his anger would keep her cleaning the house just to keep busy. At least he was paying the bills.

After eating a burrito and taco she saw her revenge. He was about 6 feet tall, dark, and handsome. She could tell he was about her age. His hair and skin appealed to her with a hot shine. He was the Mexican restaurant's assistant manager and his name tag read Shawn. He was walking her way.

"The waitress will be back with your bill," Shawn said.

"Okay, the food was really good. I'm Molly Dew," she said as she put her hand out for him to shake.

"I'm Shawn Wilson the assistant manager here. Would you like anything else, a cocktail?"

"Yes I'd like a bloody Mary."

"I'll be back with it in a minute," Shawn answered. Quickly he went to the bar and had the drink made.

"Are you hiring here for any positions? If you are can I have an application?" Molly asked.

"Yes let me get you one," he answered.

Molly finished filling it out and handed it to him.

"The manager's not here. He'll be here tomorrow. Let me talk to you now. You can come back tomorrow at 1 o'clock and finish the interview with him. His name's Jose." Shawn sat down next to her at the table and was ready to ask questions. "He'll probably just go over your application with you tomorrow. Let me just ask; do you have any experience working in a restaurant?"

"Yes, before I had my daughter I worked in a seafood restaurant for two years."

"So you wouldn't need much training. Have you ever been fired from a job before and why?"

"No I never have. I'm still hoping to finish college one day. I've only worked in two restaurants. When I became pregnant I wanted to take a maternity leave, but they could only give me six months. When my baby Angela turned six months old she still needed all my attention.

"How many hours would you like to work in a week?"

"I would like to only work part-time. I'll have my sitter Peggy watch her and Angela goes to school."

"Be back here tomorrow at one and I'll be here. Ask for the manager Jose and he'll be expecting you. I'll see you tomorrow." Shawn reached out his hand. Molly put her hand in his. Instead of a hand shake she felt more like he was holding her hand. She moved in closer and she smelled his cologne. She loved this smell. He smelled of clean soap and roses.

They mumbled bye to each other and he went back to his job as she smiled going out the door. Molly didn't want to leave, she thought he was charming.

Chapter 2

S econd Chances

Sitting on her tan couch, Molly jumped after hearing the front door shut. It was her husband. She had cleaned the apartment to a sparkling shine, but there were tears in her eyes. Still being afraid of him there was a feeling of dissatisfaction with her marriage.

Molly walked into the kitchen to grab a bag of ice. Her lip was still sore from that morning when he hit her. With the bag on her lip she watched Andy walk into the kitchen.

"So you're not a cook now? I can fix myself something frozen to eat," Andy said.

"If you want a cook you can hire one. I'm your wife I don't work for you."

"Are you being a smart ass?" Andy grabbed her arm and he started twisting it.

"No, I just tell the truth. No matter how much it hurts. And don't ever hurt me again. If you hit me you'll be sorry. Especially if I leave you," Molly said. "I'd fix you something to eat as a favor, but since you hit me and haven't apologized yet, forget it."

"I have a job interview to work at a restaurant tomorrow. It's called Peppers. I think I'm going to start Angela in after-school care so I don't have to hire a babysitter. At night she can stay home with you. How does that sound?" Molly asked.

"Good, it'll be great not having you around the house. I get the bed tonight. The sheets for the couch are in the hall closet," Andy snapped.

"I know it's my fault, but why can't you relax? I never deliberately and cruelly left the dishes unclean this morning and you were so mad. Why are you like that?"

"I need to be like that to get you to listen to me. Just be grateful I didn't whip you with my belt." Andy picked up his sandwich and went in his bedroom for the night.

Molly had an easy time sleeping on her couch.

All morning Molly was excited about her interview. When she walked into the restaurant she saw Shawn waiting for her.

"Are you here for your interview? Come follow me and I'll take you to the office." He took her by the arm and led her in the door and she sat down. The manager Jose came in and sat at his desk. He stared at her with his dark brown eyes and dark skin ready to ask questions.

Shawn sat and waited for Molly and she didn't come out of the door for thirty minutes. When she did he reached for her and asked,

"Did you get the job?"

Molly smiled with joy. "I did. I'm working part-time. I start next Monday."

Shawn hugged her. "Great, I'll show you around and if you have any questions ask me."

Molly wanted to ask him for his home phone number, but didn't.

"I'm starting as a bus person. I want to be a waitress but I can't start training for six months."

Before Molly went home Shawn showed her around and then gave her a uniform. A white polo shirt that said Pepper's. He also gave her a black one. They both decided to have a Coke before Molly left.

"Well, thanks for the soda. I have to go now. I can't wait to see you Monday, bye."

Shawn watched as Molly tried to walk away with a sexy roll in her shoulders until she was out of site. At that time Shawn was convinced that Molly only wanted to be close friends.

"Guess what?" Molly asked walking through her apartment door.

"I have a job."

Andy saw her holding her two polo shirts. "Why should I care?" He went into the bedroom and locked the door. He was cold and quiet since he hit her. He wouldn't let her back in the bed with him.

Molly felt like her marriage was over. She was sorry for that and tried to act like she didn't know he was mad by directing all of her affection on Angela. "I'm taking Angela to sign her up for after school care now," Molly said to Andy when he went in the kitchen.

He did not answer. He just glared at her.

They arrived at the school and went in the office to sign up. "Are you excited, Angela? Do you like it here?" Molly asked.

"No."

"School is very important for you. Aren't you looking forward to meeting new friends?"

"Yes you are no fun," Angela answered.

"My gosh, has your father poisoned you? You will like this school once you see all of the other kids here having fun."

The child shook her head no.

Arriving at home Molly asked Andy, "Are you giving me the silent treatment?"

"No."

"What is it then? What's wrong?"

"I can't tell you because you wouldn't understand. You don't understand anything. You're just a plain old dumb pig."

"As a last resort Molly asked, "Do you want to try a marriage counselor?" They heard a loud crash in the apartment. Molly ran toward Angela to check it out. She had knocked over her large bookcase. "How did this happen?"

"I stood on the shelf to get my ball off the top and it fell." Molly left the room because she did not feel like cleaning it up.

"Anyway we are going to counseling whether you want to or not," Molly shouted at Andy. "We need it."

"You had better clean up that bookcase or I'm not going to counseling," Andy demanded.

Molly went into Angela's bedroom. Angela was piling up the books that fell. Molly, with all of her strength, lifted the bookcase so it would stand straight up. She took all the books that were in a pile and put them on the shelf. Turning to Angela she said, "Don't ever climb the shelves again you could get hurt."

"At least I tried to pick them up. I didn't mean to. I slipped."

"I know you did. Be careful." Turning to Andy as he watched at the door she said, "I'm sorry I told you we're going to counseling whether you like it or not. Please go with me. I'll make the appointment now, okay?"

Before Andy could say anything Molly had made the call. He couldn't say he didn't want to go because it would cost them money to break the appointment. At least that's what Molly told him.

"So who's going to pay for the counseling? I think we should both split the cost," Molly said.

"I don't want to pay for it," Andy answered.

"I think you should," said Molly.

"I've been paying all the bills around here so I don't think so, my wife. What do you think we're going to get from this anyway?"

"Maybe an enjoyable marriage," Molly said hopefully.

"Is this just because I hit you?"

"Yes it is; are you going to do it again?"

"Yes, when you deserve it."

"Well I'm thinking about turning my life over to the Good Lord," said Molly. "Will you go to church with me?" she asked as she prepared her dinner. "Would you like me to cook you something?"

"No way," Andy answered annoyed by the woman he used to love.

"I start work Monday so I made the appointment with the counselor is for tomorrow morning. I know how good you feel in the morning."

Seeing the counselor, who was a woman, gave Molly hope. Never once did they mention divorce. Andy was quiet, but Molly saw him rolling his eyes. Afterwards Andy was still quiet, but somehow seemed more pleasant to her. Molly thought Andy would never change on his own.

Chapter 3

Helping Hands

Molly's first day on her new job was difficult. When her day was over Shawn approached her.

"Why don't you come over to my house on your day off? I can show you how to relax and you'll have a good time. We can go to a casino or watch a movie. Did I give you my phone number?"

"No."

"I'll give it to you." Shawn gave her the number and they made plans for the coming Saturday.

"You can go home and rest now. Thanks for all your help."

Molly took his number, smiled at Shawn, washed her hands, and went home. She couldn't believe Shawn wanted to be her friend.

When she arrived home she moved some clothes into Angela's bedroom.

"I'm going to have you start school Monday," Molly said to Angela. "Okay?"

The child nodded. At that time what Molly needed was an excuse for Saturday afternoon. She had not thought of one yet. She could say she was going shopping, but what would he think when she came home with no bags? She could say she was going to the movies or out to have a drink, but where? It was something she was putting a lot of thought into.

Molly decided that she would leave and not tell her husband where she was going. Acting like she was just going for a walk she grabbed her purse she snuck out the door. She got in her car to leave for Shawn's.

Molly met Shawn at his house. She did not feel like going out, but just relaxing. She was glad she just had someone to lean on. "I'll have to be home by dinner because my daughter will be hungry."

"That's okay. Did you see my backyard?"

"No but your house is beautiful."

"Come to the window," Shawn said lifting the curtain.

Molly saw a beautiful flower garden of roses, grass, and bushes. It looked like a labyrinth except not as high. She opened the back door and stepped out. It was so pretty. She saw an orange butterfly lift off a bush and fly away. There was an apple tree in each corner of the yard. In the middle of the bushes was a pool.

"You can come over and go swimming any time you want. It will help you relax." Shawn lived alone and kept his house spotless. Molly was the company he needed.

"Thanks Shawn. How about next weekend?"

"That's fine," he replied. A great new friendship had blossomed. What Shawn didn't know yet was that Molly had a crush on him and spent a lot of time making sure she looked nice for her visits. After drinking a margarita Molly went home.

Molly wondered what she was going to do. Half of her wanted to leave her husband and the other half didn't because of her little girl.

Andy did not ask Molly where she had been.

"Did you even know I was gone?"

"The thought did occur to me," Andy answered.

"Did a get a divorce thought occur to you?"

"No," was his only answer.

"Why do you want a divorce? How would you like another fat lip?" asked Andy.

Molly didn't know how to answer. She just said the first thing that came to mind. "I think we should start by moving away from each other to see how we like that for a while."

"You don't have enough money for that." "Yes I do have money saved and I have a job. I'm not sure where I want to live yet, but I will continue to think about it until I know."

"Is this for sure?" asked Andy.

"No, it's not. It's just an idea. How do you like it?"

"I don't. Just stay with me or you might wake up dead."

At that moment moving out did not look like a chore Molly wanted to do anymore.

Molly had wondered if her husband would ever be in love with her again like he was on their wedding day. Maybe he was depressed or becoming addicted to alcohol or drugs. She wanted to ask him if he hated her. All that she said was, "Want to come to Pepper's on Friday night? I can get you a free meal."

"Oh alright yeah sure, but make sure there's plenty of beer for me." Molly nodded knowing that he might not show up. Finally, "Do you like me," came out.

Andy gave Molly a strange look and lowered his eyebrows, saw his chance to bug his wife, and shook his head no. "No because you're stupid, he said."

Why couldn't he say he liked her? That disappointed Molly. "What do you want then? What did I do to make you change your mind about me?"

Andy dropped everything looking annoyed, went over to Molly and slapped her. Why was he so miserable? Molly didn't know she just panicked and ran to the apartment guest room and shut the door hiding with her fears on the other side.

Chapter 4

G oodnight

The week days went by quickly and routinely. Andy and Molly hardly said a word to each other. On Friday night when Molly was drying glasses at Pepper's she saw Andy come through the door.

"I'm getting ready to eat. Do you want to have dinner with me?" Molly asked Andy.

"Okay, what?"

"Chicken, mashed potatoes, and chocolate cake and we can also have wine."

"Let me clock out of my shift then I'll get our plates." This was the best they had gotten along all year. They enjoyed their wine but were still quiet. It was a pleasant quiet. They rode home in two separate cars. During that time Molly thought she could be with her husband again. Although she had not yet forgiven him for hitting her she still cared for him.

When Molly came through the front door she saw Andy sitting on the couch. "Goodnight," he said as he stood up and went in the bedroom. "I paid the babysitter! You owe me money," he shouted.

Molly didn't know if she should try to sleep in their bedroom or not. She walked into the room.

"Want me to stay in here with you?"

"No, and the dinner tonight was lousy." He closed his eyes.

Checking on Angela before she went to sleep she found the child playing with her dolls. "You have to go to bed now." Angela kept playing with her dolls and Molly picked her up and put her in bed.

"Goodnight and sleep tight." Molly turned out the light.

Saturday morning, while Andy was out playing tennis with a friend, Molly put her blue bathing suit and towel in her purse to go swimming at Shawn's house.

"Angela come on. I'm dropping you off at Peggy's house for the rest of the day."

Angela picked up her doll that wears a pink dress and her juice bottle and followed her mother out of the door.

After knocking on Shawn's door several times, he did not answer.

Molly went to the backyard fence and looked over. She saw him sitting on his bench. "Shawn, hi I'm here!"

Shawn looked up and walked over to the gate to let her in. "Hi, I'm glad you're here," he said. "Can I get you something to drink? How about lemonade?"

Molly nodded and they went in to get a glass. "Can I use your bathroom to change into my bathing suit?"

"Yes, it's the last door on the right."

While Molly was changing he fixed her a glass of lemonade and put chips and dip on a plate. He turned on the radio to a popular station and brought it outside.

Molly came outside with her hair pulled back in a ponytail. She didn't see him and went through the bush maze looking for him. She found him at the pool and dove in.

"That was a great dive. I can teach you how to do flips off the diving board."

"Okay show me."

"First we need to go to the high board." The diving board was twelve feet off the ground. Shawn went to the top and did a flip into the water.

Molly clapped and went to the top.

"Okay, you have got to be totally fearless. Jump as high as you can then tuck your head under towards your stomach. Now expect your first try to be a mess. Everything takes practice. You may have to do it one hundred times before you get it perfect."

Molly took a deep breath then jumped and tucked her head under.

She looked like a twisted pretzel, but came up out of the water and they both laughed as hard as they could. Shawn kissed her on the cheek then smiled.

Molly swam over to the side.

"Why don't you spend the night?" Shawn asked.

"I can't do that."

"Why not?"

"I need to get back home to Angela." Molly could not say she already had a husband.

"Stay for dinner then."

"Okay that's fine." It was clear to Molly that Shawn liked her. She pulled herself out of the water then dried off and went inside to get changed back into her clothes.

Dinner was great. Molly had such a good time. She had passionate feelings for Shawn. She thought about it all through dinner. Shawn still didn't know she was married and she didn't want to tell him. She decided she would leave Andy and get an apartment in Shawn's neighborhood. But she would not touch Shawn until the divorce. She was determined to be faithful.

"I'm going to get an apartment in this area," she told Shawn.

"That's good."

"Maybe later when I'm more prepared I can stay the night with you." After Shawn nodded Molly stood up. "Thank you for dinner. I have to go pick up Angela now.

"I spent the day at Peggy's," Angela told Andy. "It was fun daddy."

"Why were you there?"

"I don't know,"

"Why was she there Molly?"

"I stopped by at my friend's house. We work together." Molly listened but did not pay attention any more. She didn't want to.

"Andy," Molly said as she sat down. "I'm moving out for good this time to the east side of Reno. I'm getting an apartment and I'll be out of here before the month is over. I'm sorry but I need to be single again."

"No you aren't. Just stay here where you belong. The answer is no. I will not let you leave and you are not getting a divorce. Do you really think you can afford an apartment in Nevada working part-time?"

"I'll work full-time."

"No, I'm not leaving daddy," Angela said. The child stomped away to her bedroom crying.

Feeling respectful towards Angela's feelings Molly changed the subject. "Angela's birthday is in two weeks. We need have a party for her. We'll both get her presents and I'll get the cake and ice cream."

"Okay," Andy said rubbing Molly's arm like he supported her.

"I'm still moving out though."

"Angela doesn't want to leave. If you go I won't let you take her and you'll never see her again," yelled Andy.

"Not to laugh at you but I might when I see you try to apartment shop. You aren't getting away from me." Andy threw a pillow at Molly hard enough to give her the hint to move into the living room.

She went willingly. Molly didn't feel lonely. There was only a feeling of disgust with Andy. Fearfully she kept wondering what he would do next.

Chapter 5

Happy Birthday

When Molly came home from her job she had boxes. She started to pack all of her possessions. Molly saw that it angered Andy, but she ignored him. What was her chance of getting away from him? She didn't think it was good since Andy was threatening her.

Andy's angry feelings made Molly want to get out of the apartment and go anywhere. She ran to her car and drove to get dinner from a local pizza restaurant. While waiting for her pizza she drove to the apartment complex near Shawn's house. She went into the office, "What apartments do you have for rent?"

The manager said smiling, "We don't have any vacancies. I don't know when we will."

Molly went out of the door and went to pick up her pizza. Driving down the street she saw another apartment complex. She stopped to check them out, but they didn't have any vacancies either. She decided to stop by Shawn's house and say hi.

"Come in Molly," Shawn said as he opened the door.

"Hi Shawn, I was in the neighborhood getting pizza. Would you like some?"

"Sure."

"Okay it's in my car." They both walked out to her car to get the box.

Once they were both sitting inside eating pepperoni pizza Molly said, "I couldn't find an apartment. I don't care what it takes. I'll get an apartment in another city. I'll have a real estate agent help me, anything. I hate my apartment. It reminds me of Angela's father. And she doesn't want to move."

"Don't worry, everything will work out," he said as he put his arm around her. "Do you want to go to the movies this weekend?" "I don't think I can. I don't know if I can get a sitter for Angela and I'd like to move. Maybe some other time. Angela's birthday is in two weeks. I'll stop here and bring you some cake. She'll be eight and starting second grade in the fall. I can't wait for the fall. It's so hot out. I'll stop by here and see you this weekend, okay."

"We'll go swimming again," Shawn said.

"I'm getting tired. I'm going to leave now, goodnight."

Molly spent the rest of the week at home. She found that he and Angela had unpacked her possessions.

When Molly came to work the next day she said to Shawn, "I have to put off moving for a while. Maybe I'll take you up on that movie offer."

"Okay we'll go Saturday."

"Why not Friday after work? I can have the babysitter keep Angie and then I wouldn't have to worry about her."

"Okay we can go swimming first." They both shook hands. It was a done deal.

Friday quickly came and Molly had a fun time swimming and watching the movie.

"Maybe next time we can rent movies," Molly said.

"Yes and you can practice your diving. You're getting so good."

"When do I get to meet Angela?"

"I don't know. Not for a while."

"Why don't you stay here with me?"

"I can't, I have to get back home. Hopefully some other time. I'll see you Monday."

They gave each other a sinful kiss. It made her happy though.

While driving home Molly couldn't wait to see Shawn again. She needed to wait for the perfect time to leave Andy. Although she still had no intentions of telling Shawn she was still married and with her husband. She felt a little guilty, but knew she was happy with what she was doing.

"Where did you go?" Andy asked grabbing her by the neck when Molly came in the door.

"I went to the movies," Molly answered. "What do we have planned for this weekend?'

"Shouldn't I be asking you that? It's Angela's birthday. Isn't it Angela?" Andy said.

Angela smiled.

"Angie's birthday, that's right. I don't know where my head is. I must be tired from working. Want to know what we have planned Angie?" Molly asked.

"What Mommy?"

Trying to figure out what her little girl might like doing, Molly suggested going to Las Vegas and having pizza, cake, and presents.

Angela nodded in agreement. Molly wanted her little girl to do whatever she wanted that night since it was her birthday tomorrow.

Molly knew that would mean Angela would stay up late that night and sleep late the next morning. Molly planned to have Angela's wrapped presents waiting for her on the kitchen table when Angela woke up.

When Molly woke that morning Angela was sitting at the table counting presents and eating grapes with juice. Molly was glad to see that Angela was happy.

"Why did you put her presents out now instead of after she eats cake tonight?" Andy barked.

"Angela, you can open one present now, but the rest of them will have to be opened after dinner," Molly said. The first present opened was a doll. Molly knew it was from Andy.

"Where did you get that beautiful doll?"

"I know she likes dolls. I thought I'd get her one that she would really like," Andy seemed for once to care about his daughter.

"Angela get dressed because you're going to Miniature Golf World with me and Daddy. You can bring your dolls. They have pizza and cake and games we'll all play."

After munching on pepperoni pizza and drinking soda Angela was given a present. "You can open that as soon as we sing happy birthday to you," Molly said. As Molly began singing happy birthday she noticed Andy was not singing with her. No one seemed to notice Molly. She sang while watching a doll that sat in a chair next to Angela. "Happy birthday dear Angie, Happy birthday to you. What's her name?" Molly asked pointing to the doll.

"It's Kelly," Angela said. She blew out her candles and started opening her present. The present was a small child sized necklace.

It was real 14k gold with an oval opal pendant. Angela started playing with it and making it sparkle in the light. It was obvious she liked it. It was pretty.

Molly took the necklace and put it on Angela's neck. "You like that Angie?" Molly asked as she cut some of the white frosted cake with yellow flowers.

Angie nodded yes.

"After you finish your cake we can go outside and play some more games," Molly said. She then poured soda in Angela's vanilla ice cream and watched it foam. Molly went to get some more soda while the child was eating her small piece of cake.

When Molly came back Angela was gone. Angela's plate was clean, but she wasn't there. Andy was gone also. She hoped Angela was with Andy. Molly ran around the building looking for them.

When she entered the video game room she found Andy. "Where's Angela?"

Andy quit playing his game. "I don't know. You don't have her?"

"No she's gone. Her doll is gone too! She's probably just wandered off. I told her we were going to play games. Come, help me look for her."

The couple could not find Angela anywhere. Their last idea was to have the cashier call her name over the loud speaker. When they had her paged there was no response. They both sat at a bench wondering where she could have gone. Molly was beginning to panic. The minutes seemed to fly by so fast.

"If we don't find her soon we'll call the police," Molly said to Andy. "She'll be Okay when we find her. Maybe she just got lost." The sky began to darken. Finally the figure of a small girl ran to their table. Molly ran to her and hugged Angela. "Where were you?" Molly asked, hugging the child.

"I was looking for you and I got lost outside."

"We have to go. I've got your cake in the car. Daddy's waiting for us. Where's your new doll?" Molly asked.

"She's in the pocket of my jacket," Angela answered reaching in her jacket.

They both ran out to the car where Andy was waiting and got in.

"It was my fault Andy. I shouldn't have left her." Andy didn't answer her, but just kept driving.

Molly was wondering what he would do to her when they got home. "What do you want to do tonight Angie? Stay up late and watch movies with me?"

The child nodded at the sound of the idea.

"I want you to rest as much as you can this weekend Angie. Monday you're going to daycare and in September you're going to start second grade," Molly informed Angela.

Andy had not said much to Molly. She wondered if he was mad. She figured no he couldn't be. She didn't do anything wrong. Andy did not know about her affair. Still, things seemed too quiet. Molly watched Angela color with crayons, and her husband watched TV quietly.

She did not worry as much anymore because the plan was to leave the first chance she had.

Chapter 6

Taking Chances

On Monday morning before driving to work, Molly almost considered giving Andy a kiss goodbye while he was still sleeping.

She decided she had better not. It was just an old habit. She still couldn't wait to see Shawn that day. Molly felt all the love she had for Andy fading and turning to Shawn. She felt a sense of guilt for her adulterous feelings, but she was attracted to Shawn and couldn't stop it. She felt that the lustful feelings she had for Shawn were uncontrollable. But love was the only time in Molly's life when she felt she had no self-control.

Wearing her favorite black skirt and a white polo shirt Molly drove Angela to daycare and then went to work at Pepper's. She was supposed to be working late that night on a banquet with Shawn. She put her apron on and found him in the back stacking plates. She kissed him on the cheek and said hi. He smiled while she helped him.

"What are you going to do with your life?" Molly asked curiously.

"I'm sure you won't be a restaurant person forever. Do something great with yourself."

"I'm going to go to culinary school and become a terrific chef. I can't wait to start next January."

"Great, so you really like working here?"

"Yes, this is my future. I think when I become a chef it will be easy to get a job in a famous restaurant."

"I need to get to the banquet room. I have to help decorate. The party's in two hours. Tonight's going to be a long night. I just know it." Molly patted Shawn on the back and left the room.

During the banquet when Molly finished picking up plates, she began to sweat. Her arms were tired and her ankles ached. "We're only halfway through the day and already I'm tired and hungry."

"You know what? Just as soon as you're finished with what you're doing, clock out for your lunch break. I'll take a break too and we can have lunch here together."

"Thank you. It will just be about fifteen minutes." Sitting at one of the tables Molly and Shawn both ate shrimp. Shawn looked like he was really enjoying his meal.

"So how's your day going?" asked Molly.

"It's smooth, just three more hours and we're out of here. Molly, I was thinking we should be together as a couple. Not just friends. How do you feel about that?"

It was a question Molly feared a little, but the question gave her a feeling of adventure. She would try to have everything with Shawn that she never had with Andy. Molly answered, "Sure."

"What does that mean?"

"It means yes.

"I think we have a really good chance for a commitment. Have you ever wanted to be married?" Shawn asked.

"No, and she took a drink of water and looked away."

"Can I get you something else, a beer maybe?"

"No we shouldn't drink on the job. We have to go back to work anyway," Molly said as she stood up to leave. She picked up her plate, "I'll see you back in the kitchen. Thanks for a lovely lunch."

Shawn did not meet Molly in the kitchen. When he went back there she was not there. He didn't see her and the last work hours went by quickly. It was time for Shawn to go home and while walking to his car he spotted Molly. She was leaning on her car. "Hi. There you are," he said as he approached her.

"Hi, I saw you coming out here so I thought I'd wait and say goodnight to you." Molly kissed him on the cheek. "Well I've got to pick up Angela. I'll see you tomorrow." Molly watched Shawn wave goodbye and get in his car. Ready to leave Molly began to start her car. The motor did not make a sound so Molly turned the key again. "Gosh, the battery's dead."

"Hey stud muffin. My car isn't starting. Do you have any jumper cables?" Molly asked Shawn.

"No Moll, but I can give you a ride home."

"I'm supposed to pick up Angela." Molly was worried Shawn would see Andy at home and discover she was married. After that discovery he might not want to have anything to do with her.

"We can pick up Angela."

Molly thought that was the only option. Shawn would stay in the car, and she would pretend he was some guy who picked her up while she tried to hitchhike home. That was what she wanted to tell Angela.

Molly didn't want to take the chance of getting caught. Then she came up with a better idea.

"I'll call the babysitter and she can pick Angela up from daycare."

Molly ran back inside the restaurant to call Andy to pick up Angela. Molly didn't ask Andy to pick Angela up; she told him he had to do it. Andy offered to call the tow truck for her. When Andy asked who was giving her a ride home Molly told him Peggy would drop her off.

She got lucky he didn't ask any more specific questions. Molly asked Shawn to drop her off on the corner of Gold Street.

"Why? I can take you home."

"I only live a block from there."

"Why don't you spend the night at my house? You can borrow my clothes to sleep in."

"Okay we'll do that. That dinner you made last weekend was so good, I can't wait to have more."

"How come I don't have your phone number?" Shawn asked.

"I don't know. It was on my application, and I guess I thought you had it." answered Molly as they came closer to Shawn's house.

"Thanks for letting me stay at your house. I'm glad I didn't have to walk home today," Molly said standing in Shawn's driveway.

"You can come over any time you want." Shawn opened the door and went in with Molly. He came up behind Molly and put a necklace around her neck. It was gold with a square diamond pendant. "This was my mothers. She gave it to me since she didn't have a daughter.

My mother died a long time ago so I'm giving it to you. It's about thirty years old."

Molly loved the necklace. It made her feel like Shawn cared about her. She thanked him with a hug. "My feet are killing me. I'd like to take a bath. I need to get some good rest before tomorrow."

Shawn nodded in agreement. "If your sore let me rub your back." He turned the radio on the classical music station. "I love you," he said as he took Molly's right hand. He turned her twice and held her while they danced to the music. It seemed a little corny to her but fun.

When Molly started her bath Shawn took her clothes to wash them. He brought her a shirt and shorts to sleep in. Dressed but her hair still wet Molly stepped into Shawn's bedroom. There she found large yellow daisies in a clear vase. The card inside said, To Molly.

Shawn entered the room holding a piece of chocolate cake. He placed it to her mouth and she ate it. "That's for good luck."

While hugging Molly before she went to bed he could feel her hair. It felt like silk and her skin like velvet. Her lips were shaped like a wide heart. He thought she was beautiful.

Molly stayed beside Shawn knowing that she would someday leave Andy for Shawn. She wasn't going to tell Andy the reason because she was afraid, but next time she would tell him she wanted a divorce more firmly and he would have to understand. One idea would be to live with Shawn, but that might be putting him in harms way.

Chapter 7

New Discoveries

"Molly, wake up," Shawn was shaking her. "You have to get ready for work."

"Can I use the phone? I have to call Angela." He handed Molly the phone and she called home hoping Angela would answer.

Andy answered the phone. "Where are you?" He kept shouting.

Molly kept saying, "I'm at my friend's house. Don't worry about it. How am I getting home tonight?"

"I have your car working but you'll have to come home to get it."

"Thank you," Molly hung up. Her phone call with Andy was starting to sound more like a business call then personal. Still her relationship with Shawn would stay clandestine.

Shawn and Molly weren't talking much because they didn't have the time. They were hurrying around the house trying to be on time for work at Pepper's. They arrived five minutes early. Molly was out of breath from running to clock in on time. She heard Shawn laughing at her like it was funny. She put on the necklace he had given her the night before and went to work.

After their shifts were over Molly and Shawn decided to have some drinks. They planned to drink a beer or two, but ended up drinking a few margaritas. This drinking turned into a slight intoxication that caused them to laugh at each other a lot. Molly sat on Shawn's lap. "I wish I could stay with you again tonight, but I have to get home to Angela."

"Who's watching her?"

"Her babysitter Peggy is." Molly felt really guilty that she had lied and it mellowed her excited mood. "Are you giving me a ride home?"

"Yes."

"Thank you, I don't want to have to walk for two hours. Maybe it's time I get a new car. Let's go. I want to go home." Molly put her purse on her shoulder.

"Okay, anything for you Molly. Let's just get one more drink."

"I don't know. You shouldn't be driving."

"Your right, let's just get some spaghetti or something to take home with us." The couple went inside to wait for their dinner order.

"I wonder if Molly is getting home okay," Andy said to Peggy.

"Will you watch Angie while I drive to Pepper's to see what's going on?" When Peggy agreed Andy went quickly out the door. On the road he drove fast.

Walking up the pathway to Pepper's Andy saw red rose bushes surrounded by cigarettes that someone had dropped. Then entering the restaurant he saw Molly. His heart felt like it sank into his stomach and he felt rage. Molly and some other guy were holding hands waiting for their order. Then they kissed each other. Andy's face turned red with anger. He was so mad at that point he wanted to kill her.

Andy approached Molly and he saw her jaw drop. He smacked her three times and shook his head no at her. It was all over with. He would now let her go, but he would leave her first. He no longer cared and he said, "You will be very sorry for this." He left quickly before he did something in public he would regret.

"What the heck was that all about?" Shawn asked.

"That was Angela's father. We're still married. I was leaving him I just didn't have the chance yet. I'm sorry, but this will hurt me more than you. There, now you understand. At least I'm being honest. You see Andy has a temper problem and now I'm worried about what he'll do when I get home. Can we go now 'cause I'll need to pack a suitcase and get Angela? I don't care where you take me. I can go to a hotel."

"Of course, it's about time you lose him."

"Let's get out of here," Molly said as she went to the door. "I should have married someone like you. You're so much more sensitive and caring. I'd like you to meet Angela now and I'm sure she'll love you."

When she got home Molly quickly went through her door to get her suitcase. She saw that Andy wasn't home yet and she was glad.

"Angela, Peggy," she called as she went to her bedroom.

"Angela," she went to the living room but didn't hear a sound in the apartment.

She walked into Angela's bedroom and in fear found Angela wasn't there. The only other place she could be is at Peggy's house.

Molly packed all of Angela's clothes and took them with her anyway. She wanted to call Andy that night and find out where Angela was. She grabbed her car keys because she saw her car in the driveway. "Shawn, you can go on ahead. I have my car now and I need to look for Angela. I'll be at the Heavenly Hotel and I'll call you tonight."

Shawn nodded in agreement and drove away.

In ten minutes Molly was packed and on her way to the hotel. After getting comfortable in her room Molly called Peggy the babysitter, but Angela wasn't there. All night Molly tried to call Andy, but he didn't answer. She didn't know where he could have gone with Angela. Every hour that next day Molly called the daycare center.

Angela never showed up. When Molly finally had Andy on the phone she asked if she could talk to Angie. "She's not here," he said.

"Where is she?"

"I don't know. I came home last night and she wasn't here."

"Did you call the police?"

"No, I thought you had her. Maybe she just ran away."

"I'll call the police. Why can't you just watch her? See you left her home alone! I'll call you back after I talk to the police."

"Okay," Andy hung up. Sitting in a corner with tape around her wrists and on her mouth was Angela. Andy lied about her being missing. "You ain't missing yet, but you will be," Andy said to her.

He would not let her move or talk and was planning to give her away to get rid of her. Andy blamed Molly's cheating for finally driving him to the point of insanity. He wanted to get even with Molly.

Angela had her favorite doll to keep her company. Suddenly she was picked up and put in the back seat of someone's car. She was tied up and covered with a blanket. Angela did not know these men.

She only knew there were two of them. The car started and they began to drive. Angela didn't know where she was going and was frightened. After an hour went by she pulled her doll close to her body and fell asleep.

"You'll never see your parents again," one of the men said to Angela. He pulled off her blanket and she opened her eyes.

Looking around Angela saw that she was in a field. Tall yellow and green grass blew in the wind. One man grabbed her by her hair and pulled her out of the car. There was a car driving by and she saw the license plate said Idaho. Angela knew that she was probably far from home.

One man wearing a white tie picked her up. He started walking with her to an old wood barn. It was small and had only one door.

The barn was about the size of a large bedroom. Angela was taken into it at gun point and the door was shut and locked behind her. She knew she was in danger and lay on the ground staring at the ceiling.

Both men were tired from driving and planed on killing her in the next day or two, but not yet.

There were dirty tools lying around in the barn. Shovels, pitchforks, and wrenches were scattered. As the minutes went by the sky became darker. At that point Angela had set her doll down on a wood box and was hoping the men would never come back.

When Angela heard the sound of a car driving by she ran to a crack in the door. She started screaming, "Help, I'm in here," and she banged on the door, hard. The people in the car did not hear her and they kept on going. In the next few night hours she heard two more cars and she screamed as loud as she could. No one heard her.

Angela sat down next to her doll and she was pretending it was her best friend named Victoria. There was only one thing left for her to do. Try to get out and run away. Try to find someone and tell a nice grownup that she needed help. Those men were coming back and when they did Angela did not want to be there.

She picked up a shovel that was too big for her little body. She started shoveling small holes by a wall. Trying to dig a hole under it, she got splinters and gave up.

Next she tried beating on the crack with a wrench, which did not work. Her last option was the pitch fork. She picked it up by it's sharp points and scratched her hand. It started to bleed so she dropped it. Picking it up by the handle she ran towards the wall with it. A large piece of wood broke off. She rammed the pitch fork into the wood ten times before it made a hole. The hole was a pretty good size.

Angela fit her little body into the hole and saw that she get out. She quickly ran back to get her doll. She squeezed through the hole and then fell in the grass. She ran to the woods as fast as she could hoping the men would not come back and see her. She kept running through the dark trees until she couldn't run anymore. She passed out in a patch of grass and wild white daisies, where a farmer found her and took her to the hospital.

When Angela woke she was lying in a hospital bed. Her head hurt badly. When the nurses noticed she was awake they brought her some lunch. They even turned the TV on for her. She was happy it was all over. "When do I get to go home and see my mommy?" she asked.

"We don't know."

Angela quickly sat up and shook with fear. "Am I dying?"

"No, we found out who you were while you slept for two days. Your mother Molly is having a lot of problems. Child protective services say you can't live with her. In a few more days we'll take you to a home for young children where people can adopt you, love you, and send you to school."

After sleeping almost two days all Angela wanted to do was get out of bed. When the morning came for her to get picked up by a driver to take her to Oakwood Orphanage she couldn't wait to get out of the hospital.

Angela was frightened when a large lady came and held her hand.

"Angela, I'm going to take you to your new home. My name's Ophelia." Ophelia signed a release form on the nurse's desk, and she left with Angela.

Angela was hoping to see a beautiful palace like a mansion, where rich people would take care of her and spoil her. Arriving Angela saw a nice looking, blue, Victorian style three story house. The house reminded Angela how she felt. She had lost her doll and she missed her mother.

When Angela and Ophelia went inside Angela met the director.

"Hi, Angela, I'm Valerie. A lot of the girls here call me Mistress, or Miss Valerie. Let me show you to your room." Angela could see it was an all girls orphanage and turned to wave goodbye to Ophelia. She liked Ophelia and didn't want to say goodbye.

"Don't worry, Angela, you'll see me again. Not only am I the driver but I'm also the maid. Hopefully someday we'll get to go on some field trips together."

"Now, Angela, this is your room. You get it all to yourself. We celebrate holidays together and the local church comes by on Christmas to give out presents. You'll be very happy here," Valerie said.

"Miss Valerie, can I talk to my mommy?"

"I don't know your mother. Maybe we can make some arrangements later. How do you like it here so far?" Angela nodded meaning she liked it. "Now all children are responsible for their own rooms. You help clean it, and if you don't you either can't go out and play or you can suffer and live in a pig sty. Breakfast is at 8 a.m., lunch is at 12 p.m., and dinner is at 5:00 p.m. If you get hungry you can ask the kitchen staff for a snack. I will come and get you for lunch in a little while." Valerie shut the door to help Angela get acquainted with her new room. Angela sat on a chair and cried.

Angela thought this place was nice, but she wanted her mother. When Angela opened her closet door she saw new clothes. She figured they were hers. There were plain white blouses and dresses.

She had everything she needed in the room and she knew that as long as she was good she would always have them. She wanted to go out and look around, but she would wait until lunch to do it. The last thing she wanted was for Miss Valerie to come and get her for lunch and find her gone.

There was a knock at her door. It opened and it was Miss Valerie. "You need to come down to lunch now." Miss Valerie took Angela's hand. "I'm giving you three months to relax and get a little comfortable here. Then you will be legally eligible for adoption. You will eventually have to meet a few couples that want to adopt."

"I want to talk to my mommy," Angela pouted.

"Okay, I'll see if I can get a hold of her." Valerie didn't really have any intentions of trying to get a hold of Angela's mother. Miss Valerie knew that Angela was very adaptable and didn't want to lose her.

Several months went by and the orphanage seemed a lot like a home. Mostly during the days Angela was quiet and kept to herself. She didn't think she could get into any trouble as long as she didn't say much.

Angela liked the food there and she liked sitting by herself at a table to eat. One day a brownie hit her arm. She turned around and two girls who looked older than her were staring at her. She thought they had thrown it. One girl stood up and walked over to her. "I'm Stacey and I was wandering if I could have the rest of your meal if you're done?"

Angela shook her head no.

"You're not going to share? You little twerp. Who do think you are?" Stacey asked as her friend Tina came to watch.

"At least somebody wants to adopt me. I'll bet no one wants you," Angela said.

After that statement Stacey picked up a handful of peas off Angela's plate and dropped them on Angela's head. She and Tina turned and then left the room.

Finished eating, Angela took her plate to the kitchen and grabbed a broom to sweep the floor. She didn't want to see Stacey around there again. She wanted to leave so she planned to choose a couple to adopt her that weekend.

When Saturday came, Angela watched television until it was time for the interviews. Miss Valerie took Angela's hand and walked her to the office. The first two couples Angela met were okay. They looked like they wanted to spoil her and she liked that idea. The third couple came in the room and smiled at Angela.

Angela knew this was the couple she wanted. The woman was pretty in a motherly way. She dressed wealthy and wore a diamond Christian cross around her neck. Her husband had a black mustache and blue eyes. He seemed very fatherly.

"What's your name?" Angela asked.

"It's Teresa Betty, and this is Nathan Betty. We are looking for a little girl; someone just like you. How does that sound?" Angela nodded her head.

"We can all go to church together and you'll go to school," Teresa said.

"Can I be a ballerina?" Teresa nodded and picked Angela up.

"My mommy used to call me Angie. Will you call me that name?"

"I sure will Angie. Would you like to have lunch with us right now?" Teresa asked.

"Okay." Angela was excited about the idea. Angela got into Teresa's car with her. While driving Teresa was asking Angela questions.

"So do you remember your real mom?" Was one of the questions.

"Yes, I was with her not too much ago. Daddy got mad at her so he sent me away. Mommy lives in Nevada. I miss my mommy. I wonder what she's doing right now. Maybe she doesn't want me anymore. Are you going to adopt me?" Angela smiled. Her thin youthful lips looked pretty, soft, and friendly.

"Yes, we are."

"Good."

"We are going to take you home and get you settled in. You can start school in a week. What do you want for lunch Angel?" Teresa asked.

"Chocolate cake or French fries. I don't care." The three drove away together expecting to enjoy their lunch and excited about their future together.

After lunch Angela went back to the orphanage with Teresa to put her clothes in a bag and go home to Teresa's house. Teresa lived thirty minutes away in the town Gooding. After pulling up the driveway Angela asked, "Are we home?" She wondered how she could go home with a new mother she had just met, but things were going well between them. From the outside Angela could see a tan one story house. Teresa unlocked the gate and they walked up the sidewalk to the front door. There were large trees along the sidewalk.

Once inside Angela looked all around. The floor in the living room was brown tile that stretched to the kitchen. It was a cozy house with a fireplace and a glass door to the backyard patio. "Where's my room gonna be?"

"Right here," Teresa answered.

Angela went to the room dragging her suitcase behind her. There was a bed and dresser with a mirror. Next to the bed was a red, green, and white stained glass lamp that was taller than her and it stood on the floor. There was also a sliding glass door to the backyard with shades to cover it. She also had her own bathroom and a walk in closet. She liked the closet because she wanted to play with her toys in there. It was like a play room. Angela felt she might be happy with her new life and couldn't wait to start school.

During the next two weeks, Angela enjoyed school. She thought it was easy and fun. It also made her feel smart. She kept thinking about how she was going to talk to her mother the next time she saw her. Angela missed her but didn't know where she was. With a crayon and paper she drew pictures of all her memories of her mom.

When Teresa came in the bedroom Angela said, "I would like to talk to my mommy again someday, but I don't know where she is. Can you help me?"

"I'll see what I can do," Teresa replied.

Angela liked her time with Teresa and that was good. The seasons were going to pass quickly, but Angela would never let one day go by without thoughts of her mommy. She let go of her scary past and was ready to move forward in life and learn.

Chapter 8

Over Forever

Molly glared angrily at Andy in the courtroom. They had just signed the divorce papers and were ready to part for good. This would be the last time they might see each other.

"Where's Angela?" Andy asked. He was always angry and wanted to remind Molly that she did not have her child. The two men who kidnapped Angela were standing right next to Andy.

"She's in an orphanage in Idaho. That's all I could find out. I want to get her back, but I can't. I still can't figure out how she got to Idaho. Did you send her there?"

"No," Andy lied.

"When I find her I'll ask her how she got there. I'm calling the orphanage tonight. I think we can just end this marriage in peace now. This Friday we will be officially divorced and we can both go on like our marriage never happened."

Andy didn't want her to talk about Angela and find out what had happened to her. His anger had led him to think only of revenge. He put his hand out to shake Molly's hand. He wanted to seem friendly because he already gotten what he wanted. Molly lost her child and he was getting rid of them. "It was lousy being married to you. I don't care about your future with Shawn. These are my friends, Whitey and Pete. They are going to help me move out of my apartment. Maybe we can all go up to Idaho and see Angela together." Whitey and Pete were not the men's real names. They were nicknames because when the men became involved in crime they had changed their names many times.

Molly did not know that Andy had previously been in jail for five years with these two men. "Okay, I have to go now." Molly was feeling tired and ready to leave. She took a last glance at Andy hoping it would be her last.

"I'll call you and we'll all get together," were Andy's parting words.

Molly was not interested and she only nodded her head as she went out the door. She saw Andy's friends staring at her very coldly with no expression. They seemed secretive and aggressive to her, like Andy.

An hour later she was home with Shawn. He let her stay with him until she could afford her own apartment. "I'm home," she shouted at Shawn. "Everything's done. I'm divorced and I can relax because I know my daughter is safe. I still would like to get her back. I'll call a lawyer this weekend."

"You shouldn't do that. She's probably happy where she is right now. She's more than likely been legally adopted. It would be better for her if you leave her where she is now."

"I'm her mother and I can do what I wish. Maybe you have a point, though. We can start our own family. I still miss her pretty face and I want to see her again. I think we should drive up to Idaho this Christmas and at least visit her."

"Maybe that would be a good idea," Shawn answered. "What are we going to do until then?"

"We could start making plans for the trip. The only thing is, I know I'm going to want to bring her back home with me. I want to just pick her up and run home with her." Molly missed her child so much she couldn't stand it anymore.

"You can't do that if she's been legally adopted."

"We should think about getting married and having kids. I like it here in Nevada and I'd love to have children," said Shawn. Molly went outside to sit out in the sun by the pool. She was thinking only of Angela.

That evening the phone rang and Molly answered it. It was Andy. She took the cordless phone outside. "How did you get this number?"

"I know where you and Shawn live. It's listed in the phone book. Are you alone?" Andy asked.

"No."

"He's there now, but it's too bad Shawn works evenings," Andy said on the line.

"Why," Molly was unhappy to hear from Andy and expressed it in one word responses.

"You'll be all alone at night. Do you want me to come over or not? I can bring my friends."

"No."

"We won't bother you."

"Forget it."

"You don't want to see me anymore? If you don't I won't give you spousal support. We'll stop by to say hi. Maybe I'll take you to dinner. Make it up to you for everything you've been through. Are you afraid of me?"

"I don't know. I don't think Shawn wants you to come over."

"It's just to say hi. He won't be home."

"If you want to make it up to me, help bring Angela back."

"I can't do that."

"Why? She didn't do anything to you. Shawn and I have already made plans to go see Angela at Christmas."

"Well then I'll stop by with a Christmas present for her," Andy said.

"Alright, but you'll have to stay outside. I've got to go." Molly hung up the phone and went inside the house. She was still afraid of Andy.

Shawn was staring at her. "What?" she asked. He didn't answer her but the first thing that came to her mind was, *Is he jealous? Is he angry?* She went to her room, lit some incense, then relaxed. She lay back and thought about having her baby girl in her arms again.

She wanted to help Angela brush her hair and shop for dresses. The room became dark and quiet. Molly knew Shawn had left the house.

There was a knock at the door and when she looked out of the window she saw Andy with his two friends, Whitey and Pete.

When Molly answered the door, Andy gave her a freshly picked pink rose. She took the rose and stepped out of the door. She put the rose in her pocket.

"Want to come with us out to dinner?"

"No, I don't think so."

"Come on. You don't have a kid anymore to look after," Andy said trying to convince her.

"No, we're divorced and I would like to just leave it at that. It's too late for you to become affectionate and friendly, Andy,"

"Come on, Moll," Andy said as he grabbed her arm and squeezed.

"Let's go. We'll be back before Shawn."

"That's not funny, Andy."

Andy held Molly's hair and kissed her lips.

Molly pushed him away from her.

Andy looked at his friends and decided to back down because they were watching. He grabbed Molly by the arm and said, "Let's go. Andy pushed her into his car and Whitey and Pete sat in the back seat." Molly was afraid.

"Where are we going?"

"It's a surprise for you," he drove towards the highway.

Molly Dew was not a woman to worry, but this time she couldn't help but get nervous about where she would end up. She tried to keep breathing deeply because she couldn't help wondering if Andy and his friends would hurt her. "How come all of a sudden you want me around? You're not picky anymore?" she asked.

"I don't know," he said as he pulled up into his driveway. He watched Molly roll her eyes at him as he took her arm and dragged her inside his house. "Are you hungry? I'm making us dinner right now."

"This is not a good idea. I'm with Shawn Wilson now. We can't do this. Take me home now." Molly just wanted to get back home. She heard Whitey and Pete's car drive away.

Andy began placing spaghetti on the kitchen table. He lit two long white candles and gave Molly a glass of champagne to drink.

Molly hated this. She had no intentions of cheating on Shawn and she wanted to leave. Her first idea was to refuse to eat what he made and run out the front door; but where? It was dark out and a long walk to the highway. She heard her stomach rumble with hunger.

Molly hadn't eaten dinner, but she had lost most of her appetite. She pretended to be hungry and tried to eat the hot saucy spaghetti and meatball dinner.

"Thanks for the great meal, and I'm really sorry about our marriage. I felt we were at a dead end and you were very abusive." Molly tried not to sound afraid of Andy.

Andy dropped his fork and looked angry. Clearly she shouldn't have brought that up.

"Do you want me to be with you again? I have Shawn and we can't be. We have plans to visit Angela in Idaho."

"Go back to Shawn's tomorrow. It's over between you and me.
I can't stand you."

"Still you are staying with me tonight. Didn't the jerk know you had a husband already? Now he knows what he has gotten himself into. And trust me, he is never going to marry you anyway. I promise you. So let's have a quiet dinner tonight, okay? If you say no, you'll regret it."

In the morning Molly woke up. Looking around she saw she was sleeping next to Andy. She couldn't remember much of the night before. That was because after drinking the glass of champagne she must have been intoxicated and gone to bed. She wondered what else Andy had put in her drink. Her head was hurting so she went to get a drink of water and take a shower.

When she came out of the bathroom she saw that Andy was awake.

"You had better get home. Let's go now," He was tired of her.

Molly thought it would have been a good idea to call Shawn, but decided she'd be better off not calling him. When she found Shawn the idea was to be with a man who was more understanding. Which was exactly how Shawn was supposed to be.

On the ride back to his house Molly tried to think of an excuse. Maybe she just wouldn't tell him where she was at all. She said goodbye to Andy and was glad he hadn't hurt her. When going inside she saw that Shawn was not home. When he did come home he did not ask questions. He trusted her. The next two weeks went by like normal to Molly's surprise. She thought it was wonderful being with someone who respected her.

He kept her company at night and she would sometimes fall asleep on the bed with him while they gossiped. Marriage would come up but neither of them knew when it would happen or if it ever would.

Some weeks later, Molly told Shawn that she had found out who Angela was living with. "The people who adopted her are Teresa and Nathan Betty. The orphanage would not tell me where they lived so I found it in information from the AT&T operator. Can we leave soon?"

Shawn happily agreed and for once Molly was in a relationship that was considered happy.

"I'm going to the kitchen and make myself a sandwich," and he stood up and left the room.

Molly tried to get up but she felt dizzy. The dizziness was followed by a headache. She lay back down trying to get some rest to feel better. The pain then turned into a small stomachache.

Shawn entered the room and saw Molly still laying there and asked, "What's wrong? You feel okay?"

Molly shook her head no. "It's not that bad really, just a mild stomachache." Shawn considerately brought her some aspirin and juice.

The aspirin eased some of her body aches and pains, but the something mild was still there. Molly missed some of her work hours also. She decided the best thing to do would be to go to the doctor.

After visiting the doctor on the weekend she came home with her results, which she thought would be no more than the flu.

"What happened?" Shawn asked as he watched Molly enter the house.

"You'll never believe it." Her face was pale and she felt weak, excited, and bouncy.

"What, you're dying of the flu and the medicine is too expensive for us?" Shawn said jokingly.

"Ha, ha, don't freak out! I'm two months pregnant." Molly stood waiting for Shawn's response.

Shawn wanted to show that he was happy. He gave a smile and then clapped for her. He stood up and hugged her, "Congratulations, Molly."

"It's yours too," In her heart she wanted to be excited and she was ready to be even if she had to act. "I'm going to write down all of my plans for the pregnancy. I'll give them to you and you can help me prepare the bedroom. I have a lot of Angela's old stuff so I'll dig them out and use them. I don't need to get much."

"How should we celebrate?"

"With a cake I guess. Maybe a party. I still want to visit Angela as soon as possible. And I swear I won't try to bring her back home with us. I just miss her so much. I want to buy her some Christmas presents." Molly felt much better and all she could say to him was, "Thank you for your support. We should consider getting married now."

Shawn nodded his head in agreement. It seemed everything was quiet, even the birds outside. He didn't expect this pregnancy, but he was happy about it. Molly wanted to visit Angela right away, but because she was pregnant Shawn made her wait until after the baby.

Chapter 9

The Visitation

One year later Molly had just arrived at Angela's adopted home. It was the only house for blocks. Molly didn't care where it was she just wanted to see Angela again.

Molly was holding her baby in her arms, Timothy Dew. He was a blond four-month-old boy with blue eyes. Molly and Shawn stepped out of the car.

Molly thought everything was pretty. There wasn't any garbage or crowding to destroy the scene. It was just a large one story tan and white house with patches of grass and wild flowers all around. Behind it was a wall of hills covered with evergreen trees.

Molly knocked on the door and Teresa answered. "Hi, I'm Molly. I came to see Angela. I'm her mother."

"Oh Yes, come in. Angela," Teresa called. They could hear Angela skipping down the stairs.

"Mommy!" Angela shouted as she yelled and hugged her mother.

Angela was big compared to the last time Molly saw her. She was ten now and her hair had turned brown. Her eyelashes were longer on her blue eyes. Her lips had formed a full heart shape.

"Angie, this is your brother, Timothy," Molly said looking proud.

"How about we all go to lunch somewhere?"

"Mother, Teresa, can I go?"

"Angel, you can. Do you need money?"

"No. It's just a chance for us to get to know each other again. Let's go now so we can get back before dark."

Teresa nodded in agreement and the family left. Teresa did not go. She trusted Molly to bring Angela back.

They went to a pizza restaurant and ordered a large cheese pizza. While waiting they were sipping on soda.

"Angel, can you tell me how you arrived here in Idaho? I was so worried about you."

"I missed you too, Mommy, and I would have called you but they wouldn't let me. It was an accident. It's hard to remember 'cause I was so little. You and dad just broke up and Dad looked really mad. He started throwing things around the house, like chairs and lamps.

I was scared. He tied me up and put tape around my mouth and made me sit in a corner. He said he wanted to get rid of me. Then these two men came in and picked me up and took me to a car. They pointed a gun at me and made me lay down with a sheet over my head. I was scared but I fell asleep. When I woke up I was somewhere in the country. I was locked in a barn for the night. I think the guys, I didn't know who they were, wanted to kill me. I took a pitch fork and made a hole to climb through. After running away into the woods I went to sleep. When I woke up in a hospital they told me the orphanage was coming to get me. I still never want to see Dad again."

"It's alright now you don't have to. I'll call the police and report this and tell them what happened, Angel. Hopefully the police will be able to arrest the two men, and we can get a restraining order against your dad if they let him out of jail."

A server brought the pizza and they all took a slice. "So how's school?" Molly asked.

"It's going good. I have fun electives like gardening and home ec class. I take ballet lessons after school on Wednesdays and I babysit for Miss Laura on weekends."

Teresa asked Molly, when they brought Angela back home, if they wanted to spend the night in her home.

"Thank you, no."

"You've done such a good job taking care of Angela. Can she come visit me?"

"Why not? She can ride there with you and fly back. Okay Angel?"

"Yeah, that's be fun."

Early the next peaceful morning the family bought Angela a plane ticket for when she would go back to her adopted family. They dropped off Teresa and started for their home in Las Vegas, Nevada. Everyone was so happy, even baby Timothy was smiling.

Molly wanted to take Angela home and keep her there forever with Shawn and Timothy. She was already making plans to hire a lawyer.

Molly's fears had now all melted in the sun because she knew her children would grow up safe.

Don't miss out!

Visit the website below and you can sign up to receive emails whenever Martha Wickham publishes a new book. There's no charge and no obligation.

https://books2read.com/r/B-A-WPMHB-PQTBD

BOOKS 2 READ

Connecting independent readers to independent writers.

Did you love *Flames Of Fate*? Then you should read *Beware of a Cursed Forest*[1] by Martha Wickham!

[2]

How long can a magic ring last?Long enough to get Violet through the worst, then send her through it again. When her new husband and his friends go grave robbing, they dig up a legend. They recover a thousand-year-old ring with a curse. When she finds it she uses it to her advantage like the last ring she owned, and her husband confesses to her how he obtained it. The magic flees from the ring after killing the people it sees deserving, but when it attacks her, Violet knows what she must do. It's go back to grandma's, then Misty Falls.When she goes back her curiosity gets the best of her and she goes with a friend to investigate a murder in the haunted forest. Soon the forest is haunting her, and she is met with the killer, who wants more young

---

1. https://books2read.com/u/m0JBe7

2. https://books2read.com/u/m0JBe7

blood. Though born on Friday the 13th, she believes in herself. Is she able to escape a streak of bad luck?

Read more at https://marthawickham.com/.

Also by Martha Wickham

A Cursed Antique
Stories of a Cursed Antique

Circle of Roses
The Mystery of Frankenstein's Bride
Circle Of Roses
The Haunted Rosebuds
Emily's Darkness

Witch Lane
Nightmare in a Bottle
Midnight at Witch Lane
Herbs and Ashes: Dust of Despair

Standalone
Garden Of Desire
Led By Obsession
Relaxed Poetry

Wishes, Gems, Disasters
Woodland Escape
Flames Of Fate
Found In Misty Falls
Beware of a Cursed Forest

Watch for more at https://marthawickham.com/.

About the Author

Martha Wickham is an author from OR. She has written 12 books since 2004.

Find more at www.marthawickham.com

www.ingramcontent.com/pod-product-compliance
Lightning Source LLC
Chambersburg PA
CBHW071319130726
47996CB00002B/549